A Ripple of Darkness

A Ripple of Darkness

Friendship, love, betrayal, and loss

John Puzey

Copyright © 2023 John Puzey

The moral right of the author has been asserted.

Apart from any fair dealing for the purposes of research or private study, or criticism or review, as permitted under the Copyright, Designs and Patents Act 1988, this publication may only be reproduced, stored or transmitted, in any form or by any means, with the prior permission in writing of the publishers, or in the case of reprographic reproduction in accordance with the terms of licences issued by the Copyright Licensing Agency. Enquiries concerning reproduction outside those terms should be sent to the publishers.

This is a work of fiction. Names, characters, businesses, places, events and incidents are either the products of the author's imagination or used in a fictitious manner. Any resemblance to actual persons, living or dead, or actual events is purely coincidental.

Matador
Unit E2 Airfield Business Park,
Harrison Road, Market Harborough,
Leicestershire. LE16 7UL
Tel: 0116 2792299
Email: books@troubador.co.uk
Web: www.troubador.co.uk/matador
Twitter: @matadorbooks

ISBN 978 1803136 837

British Library Cataloguing in Publication Data.
A catalogue record for this book is available from the British Library.

Printed and bound in Great Britain by 4edge Limited
Typeset in 11pt Minion Pro by Troubador Publishing Ltd, Leicester, UK

Matador is an imprint of Troubador Publishing Ltd

For Danie who helped more than she knows.

The memories which lie within us are not carved in stone; not only do they tend to become erased as the years go by, but often they change.

Primo Levi

1

Before

When he was born the first thing he smelled was shit. Not the nice shit he would one day smell from horses, but like someone was sick and that was what came out of them.

It was the river, and the smell was the stink of excrement from a million humans which flowed down the drains and turned the river shit brown and changed the river into a sewer. Only a couple of years before, the 'big stink' had almost closed parliament, and though work had started on new sewers and drains, the fetid, putrid odours from the river, on many days, hung in the air.

He was born in Strand on the Green, by the Thames, on August 27th 1860. The place was full of once grand, tall buildings. Fifty years before he came along it was full of the gentry as well, but when King George left Kew, just over the river, they also left. And people like him moved in.

Those people, those people like him who moved in, did not bring the place down, it went down and allowed them in. People like them filled up big buildings with cheap rooms like a flood tide that seeped into every nook and cranny, and niche and corner, and rats' nest and cellar.

Except they did not ebb away. They stayed in the smelly, damp, rotten cramped dark rooms where they fornicated, where they gave birth, where they were born, where they got sick and where they died. Dozens of families in vast crumbling buildings, living in cramped small rooms, sharing a couple of privies, but where nothing was private.

He arrived in a room on the third floor. His mother, Eliza, had help from a neighbour to pull him into the dank, dark world lit only by a flickering oil lamp. He was her first. She was 22 years old. The odds on him surviving were in his favour, but with almost two in ten dying before they were five, it was not guaranteed. Eliza, and his father Charlie, fretted and worried and looked out for any signs that the little child was sickly. But George grew, thrived and was strong.

When George was five, they had Bill. Little baby Bill coughed and got hot, and then cold. His nose streamed; he had diarrhoea. At eight months old, after two days of being sick, he died. Eliza hugged George and cried.

Charlie said that Bill was 'in the arms of Jesus.' He would say this every day until Eliza got angry with him. Then he stopped, and just thought it. Eliza looked even smaller than she already was after Bill was lost. Her skin was taut and grey and her hair, tied up in a bunch, was thinning and almost white even though she was young. Against type, despite being small, she was considered jolly and loved singing and dancing. But, at this time, she was sombre and mostly silent. And when she spoke, she seemed to others to be angry.

In another room, in another big three-story house full of other families, and births, and deaths, Eliza had another boy. George came in to see the new baby. Eliza, cradling the child, reached out and stroked George's hair, "He's going to be called William."

George thought it was a good name. He smiled and nodded.

"Yes, he is going to be called Bill." Eliza looked away.

George did not know Bill was short for William. He thought it was bad luck calling the baby the same name as the little boy who died, but he did not say anything.

Eliza turned back to George, "It's a nice name."

This William lived. So did Jane, and also James who came later.

For a while, when he was younger, George went to a nearby national school. Schools set up by the church to give some sort of education to the poor. The discipline was harsh, brutal even.

Eliza would often see bruises on George's arm, or legs, and once on the side of his head and cheek.

"How did you get that?" she asked him.

"Miss Fisher."

"She walloped you? Why?"

"Got my numbers wrong."

"She hit you twice?"

"Yeh. Well, later I was looking out of the window when I should have been writing letters on my slate."

Eliza thought the walloping had gone too far. The odd belt was all right, but George was getting bashed all the time, and on his head as well. He told her that everyone got a belt, but that made no difference to Eliza. She did not like the school. She thought there was too much 'Holy, holy, holy,' as she put it, and not enough proper learning.

Eliza told Charlie that she was taking George out of the school. He did not object. Charlie left all things to do with the children up to Eliza. Besides, it was costing a penny every day the boy went in.

Charlie was a carter for the local market garden. He took the vegetables, grown at the gardens, on a cart pulled by a horse to markets in London. He started in the gardens as a boy and had worked there ever since. He did not talk often and when he did it was with a quiet, mild voice. And when he did it was often to remind complaining people that God and the Lord would work in mysterious ways. He was spare, nut brown with cropped hair so that no one who knew him now would know it was light and wavy when left to grow. His droopy moustache was barely visible, giving away the missing fair hair and the light complexion he once had. Charlie loved being with the horses, and George learnt to love them with him.

Eliza decided that George would go to a nearby Dame school. Schools that people opened in their own homes for the children of poorer families, although 'school' was hardly the right word for most of them. Anything resembling education was usually at a minimum. These were places you simply left your children while you went to work or did the chores. Places you hoped something useful might be learned but doubted it would.

"I'll take him to Mrs Clatworthy's." Charlie simply shrugged and nodded when Eliza told him. After all, it would only cost a farthing a day when George attended, and on many days he was weeding at the gardens for a penny a week so would only be there a day or so.

Eliza continued, "People have told me she's a good stick, that she gives them a bit of learning, like reading and things."

Charlie smiled and nodded.

When he did attend, George joined about ten or twelve others in Mrs Clatworthy's parlour. How many depended on the number of children working or being sick. The ages of the children went from four to eleven, the little ones sitting on the wooden floor at the front.

George enjoyed it. He remembered, in the winter, sitting in a warm fug from the big fire. He thought of Mrs Clatworthy's voice like he thought chocolate would taste. It was rich and deep compared to his parents and people he knew. She was old, at least that's what George thought then. She was small, which made the resonance of her voice surprising. She stooped a little and always wore a long, white apron and a white mop cap. She was very white, her skin almost translucent. George thought he could see the light from the window coming through her. But her voice was like treacle. Except when she got angry. Then, he thought, it was as shrill as a train whistle.

But even an angry Mrs Clatworthy didn't beat the children as much as the teachers in the national school. She never smiled but she taught the children how to keep clean, about numbers and letters, what was bad and what was good. There were no dunces' hats, and there wasn't much holy, holy, holy either, although each morning started with a prayer.

Lord God, bless this day for me and all of us.
Make it a day in which we grow a little more like your Son,
and gentle as Mary His Mother.

George witnessed her greatest anger when his friend Harry got into trouble. His trousers were wet, and she gave him a sickening smack and told him he was dirty and made him stand outside in the cold, shivering.

One day George went home full of the story of Cruel Frederick that Mrs Clatworthy had read to them.

A horrid, wicked boy was he;
He caught the flies, poor little things,
And then tore off their tiny wings,
He killed the birds, and broke the chairs,
And threw the kitten down the stairs,
And oh! Far worse than all beside,
He whipped his Mary, till she cried.

George explained to his mother that all was well in the end and that cruel Frederick got his comeuppance.

"He falls off his chair and pulls the cloth on the table and everything falls on him."

But what he remembered most was the picture of the table before Frederick fell. It was laden with food, drink, and condiments. George knew what the story was about. That it was about not being greedy and all, but the spread on the table made his mouth water. Fine chance, he thought, it would be to be greedy.

The other picture, held up by Mrs Clatworthy, that stuck

in George's head, was of horses and men flying forward among clouds of smoke and bursts of fire. The men, in red uniforms and with small, black-plumed helmets, held lances or swords, the horses, nostrils flared, wild eyed, seemed to be charging through the air barely touching the ground. Mrs Clatworthy chanted a poem:

Half a league, half a league,
Half a league onward,
All in the valley of Death
Rode the six hundred.

George could never remember the rest of it except 'cannon to the right of them, cannon to the left' which he would recite as he charged on his pretend horse around the little cottage they rented for a while, or in the alley behind, but especially when he was riding one of his father's big dray horses. Those big horses trundled, they did not charge, but that didn't matter – in front of him were the Russian guns and he hurtled headlong into them with sabre and lance.

By the time he was thirteen, Mrs Clatworthy's parlour and voice were just a memory. Now he was working at the market garden weeding, loading the carts and feeding the horses. Now he lived in Goats Wharf Lane in Brentford, just off the High Street. They never moved far, but they moved often when landlords decided to sell, or put up the rent.

George had grown into a strong well-built lad, able to hit, with a roughly carved plank of wood, the paper-and-twine-covered lump of wood used as a cricket ball, a long way down the lane. He could bowl faster than anyone as well. Most of his mates would think twice about making fun of his mop of curly hair for fear of a bashing.

Brentford had a bad reputation. A bad reputation for almost everything. The stink that had followed George since he was born was even worse here. The lack of sanitation and sewage, the overcrowded slums and the foreboding presence of the gasworks stretching down both sides of the High Street had led Brentford to be called, 'The filthiest place in England.'

More than that, it was considered an immoral place. The many pubs in the town were seen as the cause of widespread drunkenness and lewd behaviour. The young George was surrounded by poverty, deprivation and indeed desperation. But he had a lively imagination. Too lively his mother thought at times.

The wharf at the bottom of Goats Wharf Lane was always full of barges and wherries loading or unloading. They were not going far, but in George's head they were going to India or Africa or America, places that Mrs Clatworthy had talked about and told stories about. He and Harry, who always seemed to end up living nearby as the families moved around the area, would, whenever they could, go down to the wharf, talk to barge men, skim stones, talk about their world, and wonder about the world beyond Brentford.

2

Goats Wharf

When he looked back, George did not blame his mum when, one morning in the autumn of 1873, she suddenly recited: *Georgie Porgie pudding and pie kissed the girls and made them cry…* But that was the moment which started things.

George hated the verse and Eliza knew it. She was not cruel, but she did find it funny watching him squirm with embarrassment and run around with his hands over his ears so as not to hear her.

This day he ran out of the room, down the stairs, out of the building and down Goats Wharf Lane to escape. He slowed to a walk, hands in his pocket, kicking idly at stones. Further down the lane he saw Harry, sitting on the kerb scratching shapes in the dirt with a stick.

"Skimming Harry?" George shouted.

"What?"

"Skimming?"

"Yeh, all…all…right," Harry replied, and they ran down the lane to the river by the wharf.

Harry was small next to George. He was thin, thin legs, thin arms, thin face. His hair was cut, without thought, into lumps and clumps. But it was partly hidden today by an old top hat he found. A top hat without a top, only the sides and rim remained so that it looked like a chimney on his head. His skin was sallow and always dirty. But Harry's features were sharp, like a ferret, like a river rat. He was always looking through what others had discarded, always scampering from one dirty pile to another, even when he was not in trouble he was always checking for the way out of it.

The friendship between George and Harry was partly born out of convenience. They had known each other since they were very young, went to the same Dame school for a while, and seemed to always live near each other. But there was more to it than that. George found Harry quick and nimble and good at coming up with things to do, adventures if you like. He was different. The hat was typical of him. Wearing something he had picked up and put on, not caring what others thought. Perhaps not even thinking that others noticed. Once, Harry had found a discarded woman's corset and he wore it over his dirty shirt 'to keep warm.' George could not stop laughing. Harry looked puzzled.

"Do you know what you've got on?"

Harry looked down at himself and said, "Yeh, a corset." There was a pause, and then Harry burst into laughter as if he had, only through someone else's eyes, now seen the absurdity of what he was wearing.

In George, Harry found a person who he felt safe with, who defended him when other kids made fun of his stutter, or his ragged clothes. They told each other that they must keep together, that life would not be worth it otherwise. George said it without thinking, but for Harry it was a solemn promise.

At this time of their lives there was not much room for games and fun. They both worked. George at the market garden while Harry collected rags for the rag and bone man. But they still felt like boys who wanted to have a lark, who wanted to hold on to boyhood a bit longer.

It did not take long for them to find flat stones which they weighed and felt, expertly, in their hands. Then they started skimming them across the river. It was a cold grey day, and the river was flowing fast and dark.

"Bit too choppy to s'skim," Harry said. "Can't get more than two jumps."

George could see he was right. The river was high and rough. A barge out in the middle was butting into it as it tried to go upriver. The stones hit the water's surface once and then sank without a trace.

Without discussion, the skimming reverted to just chucking stones in the water to make a splash. They aimed at any stick or log rushing by and pretended they were firing at an enemy ship from their own ironclad.

After a while Harry stopped and sat on the riverbank. George threw a few more stones, announcing he had just sunk a Russian ship with all hands, then joined him. They both looked out across the river.

Harry nodded towards the big factory opposite, the Rowes Soap Factory.

"I think I'll work there. You get good m'money there," he said.

George scoffed. "You wouldn't catch me dead in a place

like that – I'm going to drive the carts like me dad – work outdoors with the horses."

Harry pushed George and they both laughed. George pushed back and Harry's hat fell off. But then it got rougher, the laughter was replaced by grunts and heavy breathing and gasps as they continued to wrestle and push each other.

Locked in a fighting embrace they struggled up and, standing, continued to try and trip and topple each other. But George was always going to win, his size and weight, compared to Harrys, was decisive. He pushed Harry away far enough and for long enough to throw a punch. It hit Harry's chest and sent him to the ground.

Harry lay on the ground looking up, "You b'bugger George."

George felt sorry straight away, but he could not say it. He stood there, fists clenched looking down at Harry. He thought it was as much his fault as mine. Why should he say sorry? George turned his back on Harry and walked off.

George wandered along the bank, angry at Harry, and still angry at his mother for taunting him. It would serve them right if he ran off, he thought. He imagined how distraught his mother would be if she never saw him again. Dad would be too, and Harry. He enjoyed thinking about their pain.

He kept walking and it started to get dark. He made his way through the narrow gas-lit alleys and along the High Street to Goats Wharf Lane, where his mother hit him on the arse with a ladle as he came in and asked him what he had been up to that late at night.

It was two days later, when George and his father came home from a day's work at the market garden, that they found some of the residents of Goats Wharf Lane outside talking to each other. Eliza was one of them, and when she saw them, she ran over, grabbed George and pulled him towards her, held him tight, and cried.

George, taller now than his mother, drooped over her self-consciously. Charlie looked around at the others puzzled.

"Harry Tompkins is lost," someone said.

"Lost?" asked Charlie.

George untangled himself from his mother.

"No," he said loudly, so that everyone stopped talking and looked at him. "He can't be lost he knows the place like the back of his hand."

"No son," said a man. "Not lost like that. Lost, drowned, fell in the river."

The conversations around him filled in the details. He listened to one, then another, then another.

"This bloke walking along the bank from Chiswick saw him go in."

"Yeh. Seems he ran but couldn't see him when he got there."

"I heard one of the barge men saw a body in the river, face down and being carried along."

"That's right. Said it looked like a ragged boy, a poor boy, a tramp."

"Police got a boat out but couldn't find him."

"Poor bugger will wash up somewhere. They always do."

George was about to ask how they could be so sure it was Harry, but the question was answered before he could speak. Eliza held his arm.

"He hasn't been home since you and him were down at

the wharf the other day," she said. "Mr and Mrs Tompkins have gone and told the police. He must have fell in after you left him. They found an old topper that he wore floating in the river."

George felt sick, he heaved, then put his hands on his head, squatted and looked at the ground. He saw Harry, face down in the river, his clumpy hair smoothed flat by the water, his cheeks and eyes bulging. Tears flooded into George's eyes, he hit his head to get the picture out of his mind. He hit it again and again, but then Eliza held his hands and stopped him.

He knew, with certainty, that his life had changed. That everything before today was small and meaningless and now there was only pain and guilt.

Eliza crouched down beside him and put her arms around him, "It's all right love."

There was no alternative for George. He had to survive, but he could not survive here. He had to escape from it all. He fell forward onto his knees and then slid onto the ground, curled up on his side and closed his eyes. He heard the noise of people around him, asking what happened to him. He heard his mother calling his name and his father asking, "What's up?" He felt men picking him up under his arms and holding his legs, and carrying him inside the building, upstairs into a room and down on a bed.

He stayed in bed. He kept his eyes closed when his parents or young sister and brother were in the room, but he opened them and stared at the ceiling when they were not there. He did not eat. He drank water and sometimes tea, with his eyes closed. He could not look at anyone. When he did, a few days later, when he started to move again, when he got up and started to eat, nothing was said about Harry. George did not want to say anything about Harry.

Charlie persuaded the market garden charge hand not to let George go. "He's sick, but he'll be back on his feet soon."

And he was. And everything seemed to be all right. He did his weeding and loading at the gardens. He went to the stables and patted the horses and gave them carrots. He ate his supper. He went to bed and slept. Everything seemed to be all right, except when he slept.

Then he dreamed.

He is running into the yard down the alley behind the cottage looking for his mates. He finds them, and there is Harry. He looks all right but is as white as Mrs Clatworthy. He is with children, playing 'oranges and lemons.' He says, "You're all right then?"

Harry says, "Yeh, course."

George is happy, "Let's play cricket."

"Nah," says Harry, "Let's play this."

The boys and girls form a line and run under an arch two others had made with their arms. They chant the rhyme:

Oranges and lemons,
Say the bells of St. Clement's.
You owe me five farthings,
Say the bells of St. Martin's.
When will you pay me?
Say the bells of Old Bailey.
When I grow rich,
Say the bells of Shoreditch.

When will that be?
Say the bells of Stepney.
I do not know,
Says the great bell of Bow.

Then, as the last verse comes near, the running becomes frantic. George just gets through, but Harry, behind him, is caught as the arch made by the two children comes down around his head and becomes a trap. Unlike the other verses the last is recited in harsh, horrible voices.

Here comes a candle to light you to bed,
And here comes a chopper to chop off your head!

Harry looks at George, his head above the arms that have trapped him, just as if his head is sticking out of the water, and he calls, "George!"

Each time George had the dream he told himself that he won't let Harry get caught this time, or that he will push the kids away and free him. But he never can. The dream just repeated itself, over and over again.

Mrs Clatworthy never smiled. But when she found out about Harry she cried in front of the children. She said the poor little boy is in heaven. The children said a special prayer. It thanked God for taking Harry away from the troubles and tribulations of life.

3

The Sergeant Major

When George turned eighteen the restlessness that had been growing inside of him could no longer be ignored. He was strong and lean; his golden, curly hair had now become fair and wavy. His full mouth and lips, strong nose and deep blue eyes gave him the look of a man older than he was. Only when he spoke, quietly, diffidently in a light voice, would you realise he was still young and inexperienced in his dealings with others, and with the world.

He was working in the market garden, but what he earned there was not enough for what he wanted to do. What he wanted to do was go to pubs and music halls, but he mostly wanted to travel.

"I want to go to France and India," he told his mum. "Or, anyway, other places in England, the seaside, Brighton, places like that." But after he gave Eliza his bed and board, he had barely enough for a few days' tobacco for his clay pipe. He was not working with horses either. He spent the day loading vegetables onto carts, or digging them up, or weeding. He was not doing much different from when he was a child.

His dad, Charlie, had a little maxim he repeated whenever they came back home together from the gardens. Being Charlie, it was a quiet maxim. "Market gardens are all finished," he would say.

Sometimes Eliza gave him back a shilling or two to spend down the pub. He had managed to scrounge and save so that he had a pair of used-and-repaired trousers and a jacket, and a somewhat damaged-but-serviceable bowler hat he got from the rag and bone man one day. The hat, he felt, set him apart from most who were still wearing the shapeless felt round headgear that working class men had been sporting for decades.

When he did go about, he found himself popular with girls. At least that was what others told him. But he found their attention embarrassing; he did not know how to respond.

It was a Saturday, not long after his eighteenth birthday, that George had enough shillings saved up to get a ticket to see Gus Ellen at the Alhambra in Leicester Square. George had seen him once before at the Empire Hammersmith and laughed aloud at his costermonger jokes and comic songs. He had arranged to meet his mate Johnny in the foyer. The matinee started at 2.00pm and there was only five minutes to go, and Johnny had not arrived.

George paced up and down. The road was full of people and omnibuses and carts, it was noisy, someone was shouting at someone further along.

He was mumbling to himself as he waited and walked. "Come on Johnny we're gonna miss the bleeding start."

"You're George ain't you?"

George was startled for a moment. Looking up he saw a girl who he didn't recognise. "Yeh, who wants to know?"

"It's Ada," George shrugged, "You know. Ada Marlow – Mrs Clatworthy's – in the parlour."

Then George remembered her. She was a couple of years younger than him and was just a child back then who sat at the front with the other younger ones at the Dame school. But George could see her features, which, he now realised, were quite attractive. In fact, he thought as he took her in, she was an attractive young woman. She was slender, upright, and had a nice voice as well as a pretty face.

"Oh yeh. What are you doing here?" he asked in an offhand way, not wanting to give away his thoughts about her.

"I'm looking for someone," she replied.

"Fat chance with all these people about." George laughed.

"Well, I found you."

"Yeh. How did that happen?"

"Perhaps it's fate," she said, then they stood saying nothing, with people pushing past them on the pavement, until Ada spoke again.

"You knew Harry, didn't you? You were the last one to see him, weren't you?"

The orchestra inside the Alhambra struck up a loud 'ta da!', to let those loitering outside know the show was starting, and to quieten those inside so that the master of ceremonies, marching onto the stage, could be heard.

Some people chatting outside pushed their way past George and Ada to go in. George stood rigid. One man swore at him as he tried to pass. But George was dazed. It felt like someone had punched him in the chest. He had buried Harry deep inside him. It had been five years since he disappeared. No body was found, but there was no doubt that he had gone.

"Ladies and Gentlemen." It was the Master of Ceremonies. "What a treat we have for you this afternoon."

The audience let out a long "Oooh."

"What a veritable cornucopia of artistry, merriment, song and dare I say glamour, you will see paraded on this stage today…" He paused and then, joined by the audience, chanted,

"In front of your very eyes!"

George did not speak. He felt he could not speak. He felt trapped, unexpectedly trapped on this Saturday afternoon in bustling London. He watched Ada, he watched her like a cornered animal watching for the hunter's next move. Ada said nothing but looked at him for so long and so intently that he eventually averted his eyes.

"But first, Mr Billy Preston and the orchestra will entertain you with a medley of your favourite tunes…" the Master of Ceremonies announced

"George!" It was Johnny. "Got held up. Here now though," he continued as he ran towards them.

There were more announcements from inside, "Tunes to make you laugh, tunes to make you cry and tunes, ladies and gentlemen, tunes to make you spoon!" The audience cheered.

George was no longer in the mood for costermonger jokes or songs. He felt weak. He felt he could not stand much longer. He was confused. "Why?" he asked himself. "Why am I like this?" The mention of Harry had unexpectedly unbalanced him. He felt physically unwell, he felt awful, and he felt guilt again.

"You go, I'm feeling sick."

The audience were in full voice and could be heard through the now closed doors.

While strolling in the park one day!

"Oh, c'mon George," Johnny begged. "We can still go in."

In the merry, merry month of May.

"No. I'm off, and you can go home," George said to Ada.

I was taken by surprise,
By a pair of roguish eyes,
I was scared but I didn't run away!

George turned his back on them and walked away. He wanted to walk quickly but found it hard. His legs felt stiff and painful. He felt like he was walking with difficulty in a dream. He went across the square and into the nearest pub.

The Bear and Staff was a large, exuberantly decorated pub with shiny brass fittings and a polished wood bar. It had big, decorated windows which let shafts of light in, but it also used electric lights, even in the afternoon, to illuminate the dark corners and the small wood panelled alcoves where customers could sit and meet others in privacy.

Despite its size, it was packed with people. There was a piano playing and some were singing. George was in the pub, but he was not sure why. He had an idea of sitting down, but there was no chance of that, so he found a space at the long bar and leaned on it. He thought vaguely about having a drink but took no action to that end. The bar was busy. It looked as if there was only one barman on duty, and there were lots of voices calling for beer and gin, and lots of hands raised with coins gripped in them, coins being rubbed together with a rasping sound to attract the barman's attention.

Time passed. George leaned on the bar and looked down at it, at the swirling, dark grain pattern running through the wood under the polish. He could also make out the fuzzy, blurred outline of his pink face and bowler hat reflected in the sheen.

"Oi, Arthur! Lad here wants a pint!"

George was startled out of his trance. He looked around to see a strong, well-built man standing next to him. He had a long, curved moustache and the complexion of a man who had spent time in hot climes. His hair was tightly clipped but his long sideburns almost touched the end of his moustache.

He looked at George. "You do want a pint, don't you lad?"

George nodded.

The barman suddenly ignored all his other customers, pulled a pint and quickly came down the bar with it. "All right sergeant major?" he asked the man.

"Right you are, Arthur. Put it on my slate lad," the man replied.

The pint was put before George and he took a long swig from it, put it down with an unintentional bang on the bar and wiped his mouth with his sleeve.

"I thought you looked like you could do with a drink son."

When George finally left the pub, it was with the help of the sergeant major. He could see it was now night. The crowds in the streets were noisier than before. There was laughing and singing. The gas lamps and the crowds and buildings and the pubs and the music halls swung around him like fairground rides as he leaned on the sergeant major for support.

"Where are we going?" George asked.

"You'll be alright with me son."

George woke that night to the sound of grunting and gasping and moaning from somewhere in the dark. He felt sick. His head was heavy with pain and, though he was in darkness, the darkness circled about him. So, he closed his eyes, but the world still spun. He realised he was in a small bed with someone else. They were big, they were snoring, they were laying on his right arm, crushing it. With effort, he pulled his arm from under the body. As he did so, the moaning and gasping seem to reach a crescendo of yelps and curses. The body next to him stirred. A deep, resonant-if-croaky voice called out.

"Shut fucking up, Digweed." This was followed by giggling from somewhere in the darkness. A man and a woman giggling. The body turned on its side and seemed to go straight back to sleep.

George was confused. He was in a bed, he had his trousers and shirt on, and he knew he was not home. He tried to remember what had happened, to reconstruct the day. But it went blank sometime after he entered the pub. Although short hazy flashes of memory came to him, he was not sure if they were memories or dreams. Did he fall in the road and did people laugh and trip over him lying there? Was he kissed full on the lips in a way he had never experienced before? Had he been carried by someone, carried like a baby?

There was nothing he could do now. He just had to lie there in the darkness and wait and see what would happen.

He must have fallen asleep, he told himself, as when he opened his eyes, light was filtering through the dust in the air. He moved his head to look around, but it hurt, so he did his best to survey his surroundings just by using his eyes. He was in a sparse room large enough to have three brass beds in it including the one he was in. He looked to his side, but he was now alone in the bed. There was a wash basin on a stand, an oil lamp and little else. Some old blankets had been nailed up to cover the window. He saw what looked like a jacket, a tunic, hanging from a nail on the back of the door.

He realised the other two beds were occupied.

He slowly and painfully pushed himself up to a sitting position. His whole body felt sore. His head hurt to move. His mouth was dry and sticky, and his throat felt like it was on fire. He felt sick. In fact, without warning, he was sick over the side of the bed, onto the wooden floorboards. Being sick and the sight of the sick made him sick again.

A man stirred in the bed immediately opposite him, their beds almost touching.

"All right mate?" the bed's occupant asked.

With that a young woman sat up next to him. As she sat up George could see her breasts. She waggled her fingers at him in a wave.

"Hello love. What's your name?"

"I don't know where I am," George replied.

The man laughed. Then a voice from the other bed muttered, "What's the bleeding time?"

The first man laughed again, "You lazy bastard Woodward," then he turned back to George, "You're in the company of the KRRC chum."

At that moment the door swung open and in came the big sergeant major that George had been with the night before.

"Hello Georgie boy. That's right you're with the KRRC, the Kings Royal Rifle Company, the 3rd Battalion. The finest mounted infantry battalion in the British army."

"Here we go," the young woman sighed and fell back flat on the bed.

"It's true," confirmed the first man.

"But where am I?" Pleaded George.

"It's our home from home lad." the sergeant major sat on the bed by George, then he saw the vomit on the floor. "Christ almighty!"

"Sorry."

"Can't be helped son. Clear it up love," he said to the young woman in the bed.

She lifted her head, "Sod off. Clear it up yourself."

Anyway, you're in the Tottenham Court Road in rooms the lads can use in London if they ain't got a home here."

"Or even if they have!" chirped the man in the other bed, still lying under a blanket and still unseen to George. The others laughed.

Like a fussing nurse the sergeant major put a second grey-looking pillow behind George and helped him sit up on the bed. Then he gave him a bottle to swig from. "Go on. It'll soon sort you out."

"Hair of the dog," the first man announced, helpfully.

"Can't stand this," said the second man in the bed, finally revealing himself. "It bloody stinks in here." He then got up, left the room, and returned with a bucket of water and some rags and cleaned up the vomit. "Next time you do it yourself son," he said to George, inches from his face, as he cleaned the mess up.

That morning, as George sat in the bed feeling nauseous and with a weighty headache pressing on his temples and eyes, the sergeant major, with interjections and contributions from the other two men, talked about life in the KRRC. They told him it only took men of good character. Felons, deserters and that sort were not allowed in. The pay was all right, and you got food, a nice uniform, and most important, you got to have an adventure. The sergeant major summed it up, "If you are trying to get away from something, a girl, a life of boring drudgery – well Bob's your uncle."

George listened intently and was only distracted when the young woman finally got out of bed, still naked. She slowly and without inhibition got dressed, walking about the room to find her scattered garments. Only George seemed to notice her. He kept glancing at her as the sergeant major and the other two men spoke. This was the first woman he had ever seen naked. And, as he listened to the men telling their tales of adventure and larks in the army, the presence of the woman added to his excitement about a different life.

He knew that he did want to get away from something. It may have been the thought of boring work, it may have been Brentford, but he also knew, after what Ada had asked him, that he needed to get away from, strange as it seemed to him, he needed to get away from Harry.

In the midst of the men's excited chattering the young woman laughed. "You're all on the bloody run. You're like escaped prisoners you are. But whatever it is, you won't be able to get away from it. Not really, not in the end." The men looked at her, then each other, and laughed and shook their heads. The young woman finished dressing and left the room.

When he got home, later that day, the full hangover he had postponed by drinking gin that morning came surging back with even greater ferocity. He could only hold his hands up and shake his head when Eliza shouted at him, demanding to know where he had been. He didn't react when she hit him with the ladle. He simply staggered to his bed, collapsed on it, closed his eyes and allowed the storm around him to abate. Amongst his leaden, dizzy, drunken thoughts, he decided he would tell Eliza and Charlie tomorrow, that he is going to join the army.

And so, three months later, George was on a trotting horse, his hands clasped behind his back trying to keep his balance. A booming voice shouting, "Steady! Let it feel you, let it know where you want to go!"

Around him the sound of an occasional thud as a man slid gently off his mount, followed by laughter and an angry shout of, "You useless bastard!" or something similar. But George had no such problems – for him this was easy.

"You're a bleeding natural son," shouted the trainer.

George felt good. He began to believe he had found his place, his purpose, his reason for living.

He learned about using curry combs and a dandy brush, and a mane brush and a hoof pick and a sponge and sweat scraper, and a lot more besides to help to keep his horse fit and well. He enjoyed grooming the horse, and the horse enjoyed it too. After all, he was told, they groom each other in the wild. Grooming is a way, as one of the sergeants said, to get to know your horse, to spot any problems, injuries, and things.

He also learned musketry, how to rapid fire, how to fire independently, and how to fire from a moving horse. There was also bayonet fighting and marching like the rest of the infantry. It was explained that the mounted infantry, like them, may not be the flash cavalry bastards with their swords and flags, but they were vital in patrolling and scouting and when necessary, joining the infantry on the ground, as it were. He felt proud of being in the 3rd Battalion and, after twelve weeks training, he was considered a good recruit. He was allocated a horse of his own. A beautiful chestnut mare called Suzy who he pampered and talked to and constantly visited in the stables even when he was off duty.

It was his second leave home from training, when George spotted Ada as he walked down Brentford High Street. She was on the other side of the road. He was curious about her. Curious about the meeting in Leicester Square. But the memory of the sickness and confusion of their last encounter made him slow down and think about avoiding her, darting down one of the side alleys instead. Had she seen him? Yes, she had. It was too late. She waved and, after looking up and down the road, started crossing towards him.

He was concerned, apprehensive, but he had been thinking about her since that first meeting. He wanted to see her but was afraid of seeing her. He was attracted to her but wanted to run away from her.

"Hello" she greeted George. "Where have you been?"

He told her. She was not impressed.

"What are you running away from?" she asked

For a moment the nausea and breathlessness that he had when she first met him in Leicester Square seemed to be returning but, like an ebbing tide, receded, at least for now. He stammered out a few incoherent words then said, "It's a lot better in the army now, only six years enlistment, and six in the reserves, and the pay is not bad. And those toffs can't pay for what they call a commission anymore, you know pay to become an officer and not have the experience and all."

She still looked unimpressed. "Like I asked. What are you running away from?"

"Nothing," he replied. There was a pause, a horse and cart rattled by, and George looked down the street. He could not look her in the face, but he didn't know why. All the time Ada looked straight at him.

The curiosity, although fraught with danger, was too much for George. He cleared his throat and blurted, "That time, in town, when you ran into me. Who were you looking for?"

Ada kept her eyes on him, she did not want to miss any clues in his reaction, "Harry and you."

It came back. The nausea. He now knew that it was fear. A fear that came with Harry being brought up. It was a fear of something that might be said that he had no control over. Something which might drag him down. Drag him down like Harry had been.

Ada could see the colour in his face drain. She could see

he was distracted and confused. She felt guilty for what she had said.

Finally, George asked, "What do you mean?"

Ada took a deep breath and said, quite quickly, as if she wanted it off her chest, "I thought you knew where Harry was, being his best mate and all. And that you were seeing him sometimes, so…" she paused and for the first time looked embarrassed. "So, I followed you that day. I could see you were heading to the station, so I followed you. There, I've told you now. And I'm sorry."

George opened his mouth to say something, but Ada interrupted.

"And before you ask, I've followed you before." She looked at the ground, at the sky, then at George, and gave an apologetic shrug.

"Why are you still searching for him? It has been years."

"I felt sorry for him," she replied. "I mean, he was always being clattered by his dad, wasn't he?"

"Was he?"

"You must have seen his bruises, his black eyes and everything."

He had, but Harry told him he had been in punch ups. George had not thought to doubt it.

"I mean that's why he couldn't hear so well," she added. "I expect that's why he stuttered a bit and wet himself."

For George this was all a revelation. He had not thought about Harry always saying "What?" And although George was not sure what Harry pissing himself and stuttering had to do with being bashed by his dad, he thought perhaps she was right. Perhaps he wouldn't have been like that if he had been left alone, if he had just got the occasional belt like the rest of them.

As he listened to this flood of information, George felt empty. He felt as though a person he called his mate was almost unknown to him. He wondered if this was true of everyone. That no one knew anyone, not properly, not really. He felt foolish as well, that here was a girl who knew more about his friend than he did.

She carried on, "His older brothers, you know, Stan and Alf, had the same treatment but they got out of it as soon as they could. Alf joined the navy. Even his sister Rosey got shaken and belted. She went off into service. That just left Harry, the youngest, to take all the punishment."

George could only think of saying, "Well, anyway, he's gone."

"Oh, he's gone all right," she said, "But he's not dead, if that's what you mean."

He stared at her and realised that what she was saying was scaring him. He was not sure what she was going to say next, whether, somehow, George was going to find himself in her story, in her explanation. But he still had to ask.

"How do you know?"

"No body's been found."

"They don't always find..."

"They usually do – but call it a feeling. He wanted to hop it. Didn't want to go back and get another hiding from his dad. Don't blame him."

They were standing by the road. Ada carried on talking about Harry and his family, and that Harry should come back now he was grown up and have it out with his dad. George could hear her but was looking at his feet and thinking about that last time at the Wharf. He picked over it, dissected it, thinking hard about every detail.

"Skimming Harry?"

"What?"

"Skimming?"

"Yeh, all right." He is limping. Can't keep up. "What's up?" I shout

"F...fell," he says. I slow down so he can catch up.

Yeh, George thought, I forgot he was limping.

We find some nice flat stones and start skimming them across the river. It's cold, and the river is flowing fast.

"Bit too c...choppy to skim," Harry says. "Can't get more than two jumps."

Is that right? George thinks, I thought we didn't get any skips at all. Maybe it was me who said it was too choppy to skim 'cause I couldn't get any skips, but Harry did.

Harry points at Rowes Soap Factory across the river.

"I think I'll work there; you get good m'money," he says.

I tell him, "You wouldn't catch me dead in a place like that – I'm going to be a carter – work outdoors with horses."

He pushed me. No...I pushed him. Who started it? I knocked him down.

"You bugger George!"

I walked away but he bunged a stone at me, and it hit me in the back.

George closed his eyes in an effort to remember.

"I turned around and walked back to him…" George said aloud.

Ada, who had been talking, stopped. "What?"

George had his eyes firmly closed, his teeth clenched and his hands in tight fists, as if he was making a huge physical as well as mental effort.

"George?" She touched his arm, as if to bring him round, "George?"

He opened his eyes, almost surprised at where he was and who he was with.

"I was saying, Harry's not dead, he was getting away from his bloody Dad."

"Harry's not dead," George repeated in a monotone. Then, as if waking up to reality, the statement became a question. "Harry's not dead?" and then he looked directly at Ada.

"Why are you still looking for him after all this time?"

"Harry used to tell me things," she smoothed her hair with her hand looked down the street and then back to George, "I was only a nipper, but he used to talk to me, about his bleeding dad, his mum, his sister and brothers, and you. He used to say you were his real brother. That you were not just friends. He told me about how he felt, what he wanted, who he was…"

"Who he was?"

"Yeh, who he was. 'Who is Harry?', he used to say. He said he would stand outside of himself and look at himself and wonder who he was. I can't get him out of my head. I always said I would find him and find out…I don't know, find out if he found out." She looked at George and shrugged again. "Now I'm older I'm going to do that, and I decided I would find him through you."

4

A Scum Of Thieves

Colonel Ahmad Arabi Pasha was standing, looking out of a window over a square in Alexandria, Egypt. The colonel was a big, heavily built man with a long black moustache, black hair slammed flat and backwards over his large head, and deep-set dark eyes. Two years ago, there was an attempt by the despotic and corrupt government of Egypt, nominally led by the Khedive, but controlled by the Ottoman Empire, to sack him from his senior position in the army. But, in the face of support from other officers, his men and, most importantly, the people, the Khedive backed down. Now Arabi was effectively the leader of a new nationalist movement. A movement that wanted to modernise Egypt, bringing to it democracy and civil liberties.

He looked down and watched as thousands of people crowded into the square, chanting, "Egypt for the Egyptians, Egypt for the Egyptians!" Word had got out that reforms that had slowly begun to be introduced were now being stopped. The British and French had declared that they would countenance no change from current Turkish and

Khedive rule. These powerful countries were the real arbiters in Egypt. But the intoxicating aroma of reform was out of the bottle, and the people wanted more.

The Colonel, though large and slow moving, was nonetheless intelligent and quick witted. He turned to one of his officers, "We will be at war within a few months."

"With the Khedive and the Turks?" came the reply.

"No, with the British."

"Right lads, this Arabi character is a Mohammedan. He's not Christian like us." A British army officer was pacing slowly up and down, holding his swagger stick behind him, on a raised staged in the main drill hall at the KRRC barracks in Winchester. The hall was full. George craned his neck at the back of the hall to see the officer.

"A few weeks ago Arabi's men killed some Europeans who lived there. He wants to take over Egypt for them Islamics and stop us from using the Suez Canal which is important for our Empire. So, we are going to kick him out and show these people that you cannot bugger around with Britain or go around bumping off white people. That we can take only so much. Then the lion roars."

There was a cheer from the men. George listened and cheered with the rest of them. After, as they walked back to their barracks, they talked about going to Africa. George was excited. This was one of his dream destinations. But he was unsure why they were going. He remembered Mrs Clatworthy talking about the Crusades. About fighting the Saracen's and making Jerusalem Christian. He wondered if this was to make Egypt Christian. But his corporal said it was about protecting British money, it was not a crusade. His corporal, as someone said, was, "One of them Chartists."

George had two days leave before he set off. His Mum was not happy. She was against him joining the army in the first place. Now she told him to desert. "Those Africans will have your guts for garters. We can hide you here. No one will find you."

His Dad, quietly but unusually firmly shook his head, "That would be daft."

He went to see Ada. He had missed her when he went back to the barracks, and she agreed to walk with him. This time she did not talk about Harry, not at first.

They walked by the river. Ada spoke first. "Well, you're finally going to all those foreign places you wanted to see."

"How do you know I wanted to do that?" George questioned.

"You talked about it, all the time – I heard you when we were kids." A few paces further, she added, "So do I. I want to go to all them foreign places as well. So, I thought one day," with that she looked straight at George with a lop-sided smile, "One day, we could travel the world together."

"You're daft," said George, but he felt excited that a girl would say something like that to him.

They had walked back into Brentford and were standing in Market Street by a lane which was George's short-cut home. He said he had to go. She pulled him by the arms into the lane, out of sight. He thought, "She's going to kiss me," but instead she said, "Don't forget we are going to find Harry."

Ada saw his look of disappointment, so she kissed him on the cheek and quickly walked off.

They lined up on the parade ground. They were wearing their new uniforms, rifle-green with red piping and black belts and bags, and white solar helmets. They had caps to replace the helmets when they were on the move, but their commanding officer wanted to see how the 3rd Battalion looked. And they looked smart. George thought they did as well. Eight hundred men, well built, upright, most with long moustaches or beards. George felt proud to be in the Battalion and longed for his beard to grow so he would look as fearsome as his comrades.

The Battalion moved by horse-drawn wagons. A long convoy of open wagons and horse boxes stretching down the Winchester-to-Southampton Road. They trundled through Shawford, and Otterbourne. People watched them pass and sometimes waved; through Chandler's Ford where children ran alongside the wagons and cheered. One little girl skipped along by the slow-moving open wagon on which George was seated. She sang and waved, and George looking over his shoulder, waved back and then she began singing *Oranges and lemons*, and George stopped smiling and looked down at his feet, willing her to stop. Which she did, as she ran out of breath, and ran out of running, and gave the soldiers one last wave.

They trundled through the crowded streets of Southampton where now more people were watching them pass. There were cheers, women waved their handkerchiefs, small boys marched with wooden sticks over their shoulders. The convoy finally made its way down to the huge docks where masted and black-funnelled ships waited.

The ships were big. George had seen such big ships before

in the pool of London, but not this close up. They towered over the men like cliffs, hissing and grunting and clanking, as if impatient to leave.

The men marched with their horses to a ship which they could see, in golden lettering on the bow, was named Inflexible. She had masts for sails but also a tall funnel. It was black and clad in iron and was bristling with cannon.

As George wondered how a ship covered in iron could float, the men were ordered to take their horses to a large crane positioned alongside it. The horses were led onto a sheet of canvas webbing, with holes for their legs, which was then hauled up around them so that it fitted under their belly like a cradle.

Then they were winched up the side of the ship by the crane. They ascended slowly, the crane stopping every now and then as they swung a little too much in the air. They hung there, confused, legs dangling, making small panicky noises. George watched, concerned, as his own mount, Suzy, was winched up. She was distressed and so was George who wiped tears from his eyes as he saw her struggle, swinging helplessly in the air high above him.

The horses were then lowered into a large hold which was strewn with straw and bales of hay where they were tethered and given water and carrots to calm them.

The men marched up a steep gangplank onto the deck of the ship. They had a brief moment to take in this colossus before being ordered down steps into the heart of the beast. The black ship had swallowed up the horses and now the men, and they all lay waiting for its boilers and furnaces to be fired up, and its screws to begin revolving and churning the oily sea water of the docks.

Below decks, in a vast hold, the men were told to sling hammocks. Then, in groups, they went to the galley to collect tea, bread and jam. They sat on the floor of the hold eating and talking and listening to the hissing and clanking of the ship, and the shouted orders on the deck above.

It was not until much later that a new noise filled the ship. It was a low thrumming that vibrated and rattled the fixtures and fittings of the craft. Again, in groups the men were allowed on deck. George was one of the first up and, as he ascended the narrow steps, he could feel the ship begin to pull away from the dockside.

On the deck the noise increased, and the view of the tangle of masts, and of steam rising in the air from the vast number of ships making ready to set sail, stopped George in his tracks. Then, with his comrades he went to the side of the ship and starting waving to anyone they could see. It was mainly the dock's stevedores, and they mostly ignored the soldiers. Then, a couple of them gave perfunctory waves back which made the soldiers laugh in an excited, childish way.

The ship headed out into the Solent under low, grey clouds, passed the Isle of Wight, and pushed its way into the English Channel. For the first time the ship began to roll then pitch a little as the wind increased and the sea became rougher.

George and the others from the Battalion, swayed and grabbed at rails to stay steady. They laughed at themselves and at each other as they walked carefully and comically along the deck. Then George began to feel hot, then queasy, as the horizon slanted one way then the other. He saw his friends lined up at the ships rail. He thought they were watching the other ships in the convoy. But they were not, and, once he joined them, nor was he.

A sergeant, also leaning over the side, shouted at the other men between his own retching and vomiting, "Keep those bloody uniforms clean!"

The discomfort and sickness continued for several days. Some men became alarmingly dehydrated. But for the rest, no matter how you felt, it was a daily routine of tending the horses, physical training and cleaning equipment. Eventually, after ten days sailing, they reached calmer waters. George found a moment to look over the side of the ship at the waves rushing by and at the land that had become visible earlier in the day. A sailor near him pointed. "That's Gibraltar mate," and then, pointing towards the front of the ship, said "and that's the Mediterranean."

It was a big improvement. It was warmer and calmer and George, at last, began to enjoy the adventure of travelling to foreign places. And there were times of quiet, when the horses were settled, and the sergeant major was not shouting orders. Time to watch the sea, watch the waves go by as the ship bashed its way forward. Times when George started thinking. Thinking of home, of his mum and dad, but more and more about Ada and, no matter how hard he tried not to, Harry. In fact, he could not think about Ada without also thinking about Harry. But all he wanted to do was think about Ada.

One hot day, George, and some of the other troopers, were sitting on the deck mopping their necks and heads and trying to keep as still as possible. "Grog here lads," a sailor, who they now knew was a petty officer, pointed at a large barrel on a trestle table. "Drop of rum lads," their corporal said to them. "Come on."

They picked up a metal cup each and filled it from a tap on the barrel. The petty officer gave them a sly smile. "It's an old barrel that's been hauled out. Got to be finished today." With that he walked off.

The soldiers smiled and nudged each other. The barrel was in a quiet area at the stern of the ship. All main duties had finished for the day, so no harm done they said to each other. They went back for more. It was evening now but still hot. George and the others were talking and laughing. They went back for more. George found himself laughing and forgetting what it was that set him off. That made him laugh even more. They returned to the barrel with their metal cups, someone dropped one with a clang, a snort of laughter. Then they started tipping the barrel to get the last drop of the rum into their cups, then sat down again, talking loudly, laughing, disagreeing.

George got up. The boat was lurching, the coast was dancing, it must be rough he thought. He held onto things to stop himself falling. The others were laughing, George was laughing. He looked over the side of the ship.

"I can see a whale," he shouted. The others laughed, "I can see a mermaid!" They laughed again.

"I can see,

I can see... Harry."

And there he was. Just his head above the dipping waves. Waving. George waved back.

Another week and then land. A purple smear on the horizon resolved itself, as they got closer, to mountains and then, when closer still, cliffs, white-stoned towns, trees and finally a port. "We're coming into Limassol," sailors said to the soldiers on deck. In response to shrugs, "Limassol, Cyprus!"

George and the Battalion were told they were disembarking here. After three weeks at sea, they were landing in Cyprus. A place none of them had ever heard off.

"It belongs to us," one of the sergeants said, "And we will be staying here to get used to the hot weather."

George could not remember Mrs Clatworthy talking about it when she recited the countries of the Empire. But then she would not have. It was not a part of the empire, it was a 'British protectorate,' handed over by the Turks a couple of years earlier, in a deal in which the British promised military assistance should the Ottoman Empire be attacked by Russia. For the British, another naval and military base in the Mediterranean was just what was needed to protect their routes to India. For the Turks, British support to maintain their empire, the status quo in the eastern Mediterranean, was most reassuring. Particularly as there was now trouble brewing in Egypt.

The Battalion trained and got used to, as the sergeants kept telling them, "The hot weather." A couple of lieutenants watching the marching and riding and rifle drill, smirked at each other.

"The sergeant can't pronounce 'acclimatisation,'" one of them said, "so the men are," he adopted the east London accent of the sergeant, "getting used to the 'ot weather."

"The men wouldn't know what the word meant anyway," said the other. They laughed and continued, from the shade of a tree, to watch the sweating soldiers being put through their marching and riding and shooting paces by the NCOs. Some of the men passed out or were sick. The officers rolled their eyes at each other, grinned, and continued watching, as if it were a game. Guessing who would fall or collapse next. As if it were the coliseum.

George was unaffected. He was puzzled why so many of his comrades seemed to succumb to the heat. He completed his training each day, hot yes and tired yes, but not sick. Not dizzy like so many of the others. His corporal marked him out as a dependable man. Someone he could have at his side if things got, well, hot.

With the heat came flies. Thousands of them. On their eyelids, in their ears, up their noses, even on their lips when they were about to have a drink. They squashed them, they swatted them, they swore at them. They captured flies in sticky tins and burnt them. They competed to see who caught and destroyed the most. But the cloud of flies that buzzed all around them from dawn to dusk, never diminished.

One day, during a break, the Battalion was called together to listen to an officer address them. The officer, short, round-shouldered and slightly bent, even though he was not beyond his 40s, had a luxurious moustache attached to his sideburns, a monocle over his right eye and was in full tropical white uniform and solar helmet.

They sat on walls and boxes around the officer, and, for a while, he walked up and down, not looking at anyone, not saying anything. He had a newspaper folded and clasped under his arm. The men could see he was agitated, distracted. He was wringing his hands behind his back, dragging one hand through the other. They speculated, in whispers, about what was going on, what he was going to say. This silent show of individual agitation and mass expectation went on for minutes.

Then he started talking. "I want to tell you about a man called Blunt. Wilfred 'Scawen' Blunt. Heard of him?" The officer looked around at the men through his monocle, like a small cyclops. There was no response.

"No, don't expect many of you have." He threw away these words in distain, as if to say that men in the ranks would not have the slightest idea…

"He's a poet," he scoffed. "Keeps a stud farm where he breeds pure-bloodied Arabian horses." This brought a stir among the men of the mounted infantry. George whispered to the man next to him. "He wants to tell us about them horses."

"This chap Blunt" the officer went on, "does not think we should be here, or indeed in Africa. Indeed, he does not think we should have an empire!" He jerked a look at the men, his monocle falling out, with an expression that said, "Can you believe that?!" The men took the cue and laughed, and he nodded in agreement with their laughter.

"Sounds like a traitor sir," said one of the men.

The officer's nodding became more intensive, almost manic, "Quite right private!".

"Posh bleeding traitor," someone said in a low voice that the officer could not hear.

"Why am I telling you about him? Because I want you to be angry. I want you to show him and his sort how wrong he is. Do you know what he has said? about you? About the British Army?"

Nobody did, so there was just a sort of murmur in response.

With that the officer took the newspaper from under his arm and held it up. He put his monocle back in place.

"This Blunt' fellow." He almost spat the word Blunt. "He has written this, 'The British army is nothing but a mongrel scum of thieves!' He shot a look of pure anger at the men. They roared their disapproval.

"Yes, a mongrel scum of thieves! This regiment, this battalion is made up of fine Britons. Salt of the earth, honest, loyal, hardworking, ready to die for Queen and country and your chums, your friends and comrades, isn't that right lads?!"

Everyone roared again in agreement.

"You should be able to trust your friends, shouldn't you lads?"

Another roar of agreement.

"People you grew up with, went to school with. People you shared your dreams and desires with. You should be able to trust them, shouldn't you?"

There was more of a muttered agreement from the men this time. It sounded like the officer was forgetting himself a little.

"Blunt has stabbed me in the back. Be careful about your friends, lads, because…" Before he finished the sentence the sergeant major had marched smartly over to him and whispered in his ear.

The officer seemed a little shocked. He looked up and around at the ranks of men before him as if he was seeing them for the first time.

After a while the officer said, "Yes, well, very good, carry on." And with that he turned and walked back to the officers' tents. The sergeant major dismissed the men with a look that betrayed nothing of the last few minutes.

Most of the men were sniggering, some wondered whether the officer was on the booze or if the heat had got to him, or both. But George could not stop thinking about what he said about being a friend. About a friend stabbing you in the back.

He walked and thought. And then, without warning, a half covered, half buried memory pushed its way up through the accumulation of the roots and dirt of time.

He is sitting on the floor......

I'm on the floor. Harry's next to me. I feel a warm, wet sensation around my arse. I look down and see a spreading pool of water.

"Miss Clatworthy! Miss Clatworthy, Harry's wet himself," I shout.

There is a gurgle of laughter among the others.

She wades through the children sitting on the floor. She gets to Harry, sees the wet stain and smacks him hard on the side of the head. He topples over and then she grabs hold of his ear. She drags him up by the collar, pee dripping from his short trousers, and pushes him towards the door.

As she opens it an icy blast blows in. Harry stands outside for an hour.

This was different. Different from when he had thought

about it before. Before, he had been a mere bystander. An observer. Now he was a central character. The one who had initiated the events that had led to the action. The wet pool would have been discovered, probably. But George was a crucial figure in making sure it was. And now, as he recalled this event, he could not think why he did what he did.

Time was up for preparations. Now, it was time for action. It was July. It was hot.

The 3rd Battalion KRRC were ordered to the docks at Limassol. Another big ship, this time HMS Sultan, another boarding, the horses alarmed again, the men unsure, expectant. This time at least it was a quick crossing on a calm sea. The next day, George, and others from his company, went on deck and found themselves surrounded by ships of all sizes, and looking to land they saw a large city of minarets domed buildings, and huge fortifications.

They were looking at Alexandria.

The city was a mix of Eastern and European architecture, with broad boulevards and wide squares, but also with a maze of smaller streets and alleys leading off from the main thoroughfares. It had a population of two hundred thousand, of which fifty thousand were Europeans. The Khedives' palace was here, but by now Colonel Arabi Pasha and his nationalist army had fortified the city. The earlier unrest directed at Europeans had subsided as nationalist forces policed the streets. Arabi knew that the riots, which were grossly exaggerated in the European press, would provide a pretext for the British to intervene on the side of the Khedive and the Turks. And, looking out from the huge walls at the fleet of ships now outside the harbour, here indeed they were.

A day passed. Admiral Seymour, commanding the Royal Navy's ironclad fleet, was ordered to intervene if it looked as though the Egyptian nationalists were reinforcing their shoreline positions. By July 11th it looked that way to him.

George, with the rest of his company, were below decks, sorting and cleaning equipment, waiting for their first mugs of tea, bread and bacon. It was 7.00 am. A flag was hoisted on the admiral's ship, Inflexible, instructing HMS Alexandra to lob a shell into the Ras-el-Tin shore battery. The explosion stopped George and his comrades in their tracks. They looked at each other with a 'here we go' expression on their faces.

Another flag from the admiral signalled all ships to attack the batteries. A huge roar came from the deck of the Sultan above them. The ship rolled. It had fired one of its eighteen-ton guns at the nearest shore battery. The men below could now hear a continues thump and bang of cannon fire like rolling thunder. Shells from twenty-five-ton, eighteen-ton, twelve-ton, nine-ton guns all sped towards the shore batteries of Alexandria. And some overshot. Some fell on houses, markets, shops, on theatres, on coffee houses, on people.

Every few minutes their own ship would fire and roll so that, after a time, they got used to it. They could also hear a different sort of boom and crash. It was the shore batteries replying. Firing at the British fleet.

But this was an uneven battle. The British ships and guns were the most modern in the world. Rifled, the guns threw high velocity shells up to two miles with devastating effect. The shore batteries were old smooth-bored guns with untrained men operating them. After ten hours bombardment the Egyptian forces had withdrawn.

George had found the regular discharge of the ship's guns, followed by the roll, then the ship righting itself, then the pause, then the whole cycle repeating, oddly comforting. As the hours passed it was as if nothing else was happening, and that nothing else would ever happen. Here he was, sitting with his mug of tea in an endless noisy, repeating ritual, knowing, while it went on, nothing else could. He was there and nowhere else. There was no past and no future, and that satisfied him.

"Penny for them George?" It was his corporal who had sat down next to him. He liked his corporal but was annoyed that on this occasion he had broken his reverie. The corporal was shorter than George, ruddy featured with striking blue eyes and straw-coloured hair. He had the usual droopy moustache. He spoke in a pleasant West Country accent that reminded people of a bucolic rural idyll. Even in the heat of Cyprus, even in the noise of a devastating barrage. The corporal, a teetotaling Methodist with a passion for justice and fairness, was a reassuring, calm presence for the men.

George just shrugged at his question. But the corporal was not really looking for an answer. "You know we're here for a purpose, don't you? We're not here just for the ride my son."

As if by arrangement, just as the corporal was speaking, the barrage came to a sudden halt. The men looked around and up, as if they could see through the sides of the ships, for a sign of what was coming next.

"Right my sonner's," said the corporal, "I think it will be our turn soon to defend the honour of dear old England. And the interests of the rich."

There was laughter from the men nearby, "Why do you say that corp?" One of them asked. "I mean, about the rich. I thought we were here to help the Europeans from being murdered."

"Yes, we are, but there are Egyptians being murdered as well, are we here to help them?"

"I suppose we are corp," someone answered.

The corporal smiled and shook his head, "No. We're here to save Egypt from the Egyptians, not so save Egyptians. We're here to keep our chums, the Turks, in charge, because that keeps British money safe. Because that makes sure we can use the Suez Canal without charge. Who knows what would happen if the Egyptians ended up running their own country!" He laughed to show it was irony, then paused. "Sorry me lovelies, this is not a crusade to free people. We're here to keep the rich, rich and the poor in their place."

A sergeant, who had come into the bunk room and listened to the corporal for a few minutes, raised his voice. "All right corporal, that's enough. Don't go upsetting the lads."

The corporal had not realised the sergeant was in the room. He looked quickly up and then slowly nodded his head in agreement.

"Any rate, we're here for queen and country aren't we my sonner's?" the corporal said to the men. The response was muted. The mood in the room was reflective. George thought about what the corporal had said. He wasn't sure he understood it all. But, anyway, he was not ready to consider the moral implications of being there. He was simply glad he was, and not in Brentford.

The next day, Admiral Seymour ordered marines and a detachment of blue jackets, an armed navy formation, to land in the dock area of Alexandria. They found the city almost deserted. The Egyptian army had withdrawn towards Cairo. Many of the residents had left the city in the face of the bombardment. Others were simply keeping out of the way. After another day, George and two KRRC companies, and their horses, were offloaded on the harbour side. They commandeered some nearby buildings and set up tents. Then they waited for orders.

It was late July; the bridgehead the British had established around the port area had not expanded. The men remained in the protected area seeking shade as the heat built up every day from sunrise.

But, on one of those late July days orders were given. George's company was told it was time to 'show the flag' and restore a bit of calm in the city.

They were told to trot through the city streets in fours or fives with their rifles on their backs and bayonets by their sides. They were to take riding whips as well, not for the horses, but to use on the locals if anyone 'takes liberties.'

"Break up any groups you see hanging around lads," they were told. "They won't hang around once they see you 'orrible lot!" The men laughed; they were confident that no one would challenge them. After all, they were armed, on horseback, and they were British.

George rode by his corporal and told him he was glad they were at last doing something.

The corporal shook his head, "Not so sure me sonner. Don't know what we are supposed to achieve riding around the streets all exposed like."

For George, hearing the words of the corporal whose judgement and wisdom he so admired made him reflect. Suddenly the boredom-relieving patrol he was looking forward to had taken on a dangerous dimension.

The five men in Gorge's patrol rode out into the broad and long Alexandria square. A square with an elongated, narrow garden area running through the middle, surrounded by elegant European-style buildings. Except now, many of the buildings were in ruins. The square itself was pockmarked with craters and it seemed as if all the trees in the ornamental gardens had been shattered.

George was shocked, "I thought the bombardment was to destroy the fortresses on the coastline."

The corporal sighed and looked around at the devastation, "Those big shells overshoot targets. And this is the result."

The little patrol rode through a deserted wasteland, taking in what their powerful, modern weapons could now do to buildings. And, they realised, when every now and then they found small groups of people scrabbling at piles of rubble, looking for buried loved ones and friends, what it could do to people.

They swung off one of the main squares and moved into a labyrinth of narrow streets with white one- or two-storey buildings either side. It was now early afternoon, hot and quiet. They rode deeper into the maze of streets with just the sound of the horses' hooves on the stone. There seemed to be no one around; it was unnerving.

George was at the front when they rounded a corner and, suddenly, before them was a group of young men. One of them shouted, "God bless Queen Victoria!"

The men were wearing long white gowns and red tarbooshes. There was about twenty of them and they were blocking the narrow street.

As he was at the front of the patrol, and saw the man who shouted, George felt he needed to do something to reduce the tension. He halted and as he waited for the rest of the patrol to catch up with him, he smiled and said, "That's right mate, now off you go."

But the young men stood and watched.

The corporal trotted up to the side of George. "I smell trouble."

"Corporal." It was one of the other men in the patrol. The corporal looked around. The man nodded his head behind them. Another group of young men, in similar outfits, had appeared in their rear. They were trapped.

The corporal spoke quietly and calmly, "All right lads, just walk the horses slowly down the road towards them in front of us. Make sure your riding whips are at the ready, but don't make it obvious."

They had taken no more than two steps when a stone hit a horse. It rose on its hind legs, wicking with fear, the trooper struggling to calm it. Then more stones, not just from the men in front of the patrol but those behind and from some of the windows and balconies around them.

The horses were frightened, it was happening quickly and

in a confined space. The corporal shouted, "Charge them with the whips lads. Then quick as you can, off down the street!"

They crashed into the men ranged across the street in front of them. One of them tried to grab hold of the bridle on George's horse but he struck him across the head with his riding whip, and the man let go. The stone throwing stopped for a moment as the British and the Egyptians became jumbled together in a chaotic free-for-all. The riders pushed and slapped their way through the group and then galloped off down the road, pursued by shouts and stones.

After a few minutes galloping, skidding, slipping and sliding along the stony street, they stopped in an empty square. No one was badly hurt, nor any of the horses, but now they knew what to expect.

The way back to the bridgehead area meant going through more narrow streets and squares, so they stashed their whips and drew their swords. They wanted to show they were not to be messed with. They wanted to hide their fear. The corporal was now disorientated. He was not sure which way to go. He also knew that galloping the horses would be dangerous. They could rush into a trap. The horses could slip and slide again on the stony street. They could crash into walls on the narrow, sharp corners. They could throw their riders who would be quickly overwhelmed by the mobs on the street. But who could blame these people for wanting revenge after the destruction wrought by the bombardment on their homes? The soldiers had to tread carefully.

The journey back seemed to George to be mournful – the sound of the horses' hooves, moving slowly on the narrow street stones, echoing back from the white walled buildings either side of them. The suffocating silence, the eyes behind shutters, watching. The corporal said, under his breath, "Not far lads, not far." But to them it felt like a million miles.

The hard street stone, the hard sun, the black sharp shadows into which they could hardly see. It felt marble cold in the heat. George lost himself. Time stopped. It was like he had always been there and will always be there on those hot, cold streets – waiting for death.

Everything was slow, as if they couldn't move faster even if they wanted too. Every corner they came to increased the fear and tension. They went down those streets, twisting their necks around to all sides like owls looking for mice – but they were the ones being hunted.

Suddenly, down one street, a great noise went up. They couldn't see anyone, but there was screaming and shouting and banging from behind windows and shutters and doors. Whatever that noise was supposed to do, it shook George out of his morbid trance. He gripped his sword and was ready to charge.

The corporal said, "Just a lot of mafficking about my lovers, take no notice." Then they heard another, different, commotion in front of them, and around the corner came a company of marines, bayonets fixed, and looking like they meant business.

The corporal went up to the sergeant major in charge of the company and made a report. The sergeant major nodded and ordered the marines to move forward. As they passed, one of George's squad said he could have kissed them. Then they rode out into an open square, free and wide, talking and laughing in relief, before finally making it back to the bridgehead.

As they rode back, George realised that he could have easily killed one of those young Egyptians. That the fear and the anger he felt meant that he would have had no compunction – that he would have taken his bayonet to one of them, or simply grabbed one by the hair and dragged him down the street as he rode away. He wished he had. He wanted revenge, but he was not sure for what. The thought surprised him. He didn't know he had these feelings in him. And then, he wondered, when push comes to shove, could he really do it?

That night George had the dream – the dream with children, and oranges and lemons – but it had changed, like dreams do, into something else. This time the children were throwing stones at him, and Harry was in an open window, high up and framed by white walls, throwing stones at him the hardest. Then Harry threw an even bigger stone at George. It came slowly towards him. He had time to duck it and it went over his head, and when he looked around, he saw it sink into dark, cold, deep water.

Within a few days Colonel Arabi withdrew his forces further towards Cairo and made ready to defend that city. Alexandria became calmer. George and the Battalion were told they would be staying in Egypt for the foreseeable future. They settled down in quarters and made their life as comfortable as possible. George kept busy. He thought about Ada and tried not to think about Harry. After a while it looked as though the Battalion might be relieved and shipped home, until news of a terrible tragedy reached them, and things changed again.

5

Ali

The Battalion's stable boy, Ali, was hardly a boy. In fact, he was older than George. He was tall, strong and athletic looking. Dark skinned with a dark beard and even white teeth. His eyes betrayed a mischievous nature. He was always laughing, and singing, or mimicking animals and birds. He could impress with some conjuring tricks as well. He was a favourite of the Battalion and in the months they were billeted in Alexandria, George, and Ali forged a strong friendship.

After the horses had been seen to, the two of them would sit, and talk and laugh over a cup of chai. Chatting about this and that, about families, friends, about each other.

Ali would talk to George about what he had read, what he had learned.

"Have you read *One thousand and one Nights*?" Ali asked. "The stories about Sinbad and Scheherazade and Prince Ahmed? What about Omar Khayyám?"

He told George about the Quran, "It's like your bible," he said.

He asked who the great writers and poets were in England. George felt foolish. He realised he only knew music hall jokers and their limericks. "There was a great writer called Shakespeare, but I don't know any of it."

"Ah yes," said Ali, "I have heard of this man Shakespeare. He writes of love and war and betrayal."

Ali could see that George had nothing to say, could see he was embarrassed about his ignorance. He put his arm around him. "You cannot know what you have not learnt. There is no shame in this."

George wiped his eyes with the back of his hand. Sniffed. And then put his hand on Ali's embracing arm.

Months passed and George and his company, settled into a routine of drills, equipment cleaning, and patrols. But being able to talk to and be with Ali, made this time more than bearable, it became special, an experience that George had never known before. He still thought about home Ada, his mum and dad and inevitably, like a chronic pain he could never rid of Harry. But these days listening to, and learning from Ali, became a reason for existence in itself.

Then there was a letter.

It was his first letter from home. His mum and dad could not write and were too embarrassed to ask someone to do it for them. No, this letter, he was excited to see, was from Ada.

He found a quiet place to sit near the dockside and read it. He carefully took it out of its envelope, unfolded it, and just took in the neat, blue ink writing and felt the three pages of soft paper in his hands. He looked at the end first. It said, 'From your affectionate Ada.'

He smiled. Now after being glad he was away from Brentford, he wanted to be there because that's where Ada was.

The letter began with a few usual pleasantries. 'Hope all is well with you. All's well here. I met your mum down at the market and she said to send her very best wishes.'

George smiled at the ordinariness of being at the market and the two women chatting. He realised how much all these normal things had now become forgotten by him. Now he was in such different circumstances and in such a different place. He went back to the letter, and quickly realised the true motivation behind Ada writing it.

'Harry has been seen. He's been seen a few times now. Hanging around the station and the Brick Makers Arms.'

George sighed, shook his head and looked up to the sky. "For Christ's sake. How can you know it's him after all these years?"

'It was him,' she wrote, almost in answer, 'because Deirdre knew him really well and said you can tell by his eyes and his nose and chin.'

George could not think who Deirdre was at first, then remembered her being one of the girls living down the lane. Must be a friend of Ada's he thought. But it was clear that all this information from Ada was second hand.

'Can't work out why he doesn't come back though,' she wrote. 'His dad is dead now and his mum would be ever so happy to see he was alive.'

George was frustrated, annoyed. He spoke out loud: "Ada, he hasn't come back home because it's not him." George knew that was the obvious answer. He knew she was so desperate for Harry to still be alive that she was blinded by the truth of the matter.

'One more thing,' Ada wrote. 'Deirdre got one of the lads, Sid I think it was, to go up to him the second time he was seen. He went up to him and said, "Harry?" He looked at Sid and said "George?" and then walked off. So he thought Sid was you and when he saw he wasn't he left.'

There were shouted orders from somewhere in the encampment. Seagulls reeled and squawked around the port area. The sea lapped gently against the breakwaters. George stared at the horizon, hardly daring to read another line. He felt his blood pulsing in his ears.

He read it again and thought no, he is saying his name is George. He's not thinking it's me. It all depends how it was said, she wants it to be Harry so that's the way she is telling it.

Even so, the letter affected him.

The next news he heard made him, and his Battalion, think they might, at last, be going home. They were called together in Alexandria Square, where they formed ranks in front of a stand, on which Admiral Seymour and their commanding officer were standing.

Admiral Seymour, in full uniform, tall and ramrod straight with his head tilted back a little so he could see the men under the peak of his hat, cleared his throat and started to say something. But most of the men could hardly hear him. His words were carried away on the wind. One of the officer's hurried to the stand and informed the Admiral that he could not be heard.

After a brief discussion it was agreed that his words would be relayed by a couple of the loudest sergeant's in the Battalion.

Admiral Seymour, despite his size, and his bushy moustache and sideburns, had a surprisingly reedy voice. His accent was cut-glass aristocratic and with a slight impediment, so he was not easy to understand.

George's version came via a cockney Regimental Sergeant Major who managed to mangle many of the words. With another sergeant major shouting out a version to the ranks further along, it became difficult to fully understand it all, but the essence was clear. A British expeditionary force, (in the RSM's words an 'exhibition force') had, in a daring raid, seized the Suez Canal, (the RSM's translation was 'squeezed 'the Suez Canal'). Then, ten thousand troops had been landed and marched on Cairo. After a fierce battle the Egyptian nationalist army was put to flight (or in the RSM's version 'put to fright') and Cairo had been taken. The ranks were ordered to give three cheers. Which they did, wholeheartedly, thinking that this meant home.

But they did not go home, at least not then.

Arabi and the nationalist uprising had been defeated, but the British stayed in Egypt to stabilise the Khedive and Turkish rule and protect British interests. They reorganised and trained a new Egyptian/Turkish army that, as well as policing the country, would now have to contend with an uprising in the Egyptian province of Sudan.

An Egyptian/Turkish task force, led by William Hicks, a British officer, formally a colonel in the Indian Army, was sent into Sudan to crush the revolt. One thing was certain, after the deployment of a large army and navy to defeat the Egyptian nationalists, the British had no desire to become further embroiled in the region's problems. Better that the Egyptians were trained and equipped to do their own dirty work. Just as long as the country was stable under the authoritarian rule of the Khedive and Turks, and just as long as it paid its debts, which was all that mattered.

None of this was of any consequence to George and his comrades in the KRRC. They were now nearing the end of their first year in Alexandria and were wondering when they would be going home. For George it was different. Here, away from Brentford, the unsettling thoughts he had been dogged by seemed to have eased over time. Even the nightmares had receded. His friendship with Ali was something special and new to him. It was only the thought of being separated from Ada that confused the matter. He missed her and wondered how they could be together without being back in that place full of dreadful memories.

On January 17th 1884, there was a short article on page eight of the West London Observer, with the headline:

'Mystery of Harry Tompkins
Did boy drown or run away?
Sightings in Brentford, Acton and Isleworth.
Mother desperate to find son missing for over 10 years.'

The article briefly recounted the events of a decade before when the boy went missing, including eyewitness accounts of his body floating in the Thames.

'Another child lost to the river,' it stated, reminding its readers of the death toll of infant and youth drownings over the years.

'But now a number of people in the boroughs along the river, claim they have seen Harry Tompkins, alive and well. A former friend of the boy, Ada Marlow, went to the police and asked them to re-open the case given the sightings. The police have refused, stating that the witness evidence at the time clearly pointed to the boy being drowned.

The boy's mother has stated that she has always thought he was alive but perhaps had been injured and had lost his memory. Miss Marlow has told this journal that she also believes he is alive but would not speculate on his reasons for staying away from home for so long. She, and a number of other residents in the Brentford and adjacent areas, are asking the police to reconsider their position and open the case.'

Ada had become an apprentice milliner, which was a step up for a girl of her class. She had secured work at Mrs Dobson's shop in Twickenham. Ada had done some sewing and clothes-making for Mrs Dobson who was impressed, and who offered her an apprenticeship.

During a short break from her work, Ada ran to nearby tobacconist and newspaper shop and brought a copy of the Observer. The reporter she had spoken to told her it would be in that day's edition. Sure enough, there it was, and with her name in print. She wanted to tell someone, to show them the article. She was the only person she knew, apart from Len Skinner, who had ever had their name in print in a newspaper. And Len was only in the paper when he was sentenced for pinching lead from a church roof, so that didn't really count. She was so proud. She showed her workmates, her friends and her mum and dad, who were all clearly impressed. But she told each of them, "I'm doing this to help find Harry. Perhaps the police will re-open the case. Perhaps others will look for him and find him. Perhaps now he will come forward."

Ada bought another copy of the Observer and cut out the article to include with her letter to George. She had started to write it when there was a knock at her door. It was Mrs Tompkinson and a number of others who Ada knew, including Deirdre. Mrs Tompkinson was out of breath, her voice was strangled, shrill, emotional. She was holding an envelope tightly in her hand and held it out to Ada. "It's from Harry," she blurted.

Ada knew Mrs Tompkins couldn't read so asked her how she knew it was from him.

She said "I learnt his name. I always knew what his name looked like in writing and there it is, at the bottom. Read it Ada love, go on."

For a moment, standing in the door of her home, Ada felt vindicated. A letter from Harry. I knew it she thought. But then other thoughts and emotions crowded in. Mrs Tompkinson stood in front of her, shaking, holding the envelope out.

"But how…?"

"It was pushed under me door Ada. Found it just now."

"Why bring it here?"

"You've been doing all the business about Harry still being around and you're a bright girl so I thought you can read it for me."

Ada took it, read it quickly and quietly to herself first,

then looked at Mrs Tompkins and the rest and said, "Out loud?"

"Yeh."

"All right then."

'Dear Mum. Don't tell anyone about this letter. Sorry I have been away so long. I'll tell you about it when I see you. I'm afraid to come home because all the people now know, and I feel ashamed.

I haven't got any money. I'm hungry. Please leave five bob in a tin or something on the doorstep last thing at night. Don't tell anyone and don't try and see me – not ready to see you yet.

I miss you and sorry about Dad. Miss him as well.

Harry.'

Ada looked at Mrs Tompkins. "This ain't from Harry," she said, with a hint of anger in her voice.

"Why not?"

"Well Harry knew you couldn't read love so he's not going to send you a letter asking you not to tell anyone about it is he? He would know you would need help to read it".

Harry's mother looked puzzled for a few moments. Then understood. Then her faced puffed up, went red and she started to cry. Ada took her into the house away from the others.

"Honestly love," Ada said. "Would Harry really miss his dad?"

Ada thought it was odd that Mrs Tompkins did not react to that. She simply seemed not to understand the point she was making. "Look it's someone who has heard about all this and is after making a few bob from you," Ada added.

Mrs Tomkins started to cry, and Ada thought again about

her campaign to find Harry.

For Ada, the crusade to find Harry had become the most important thing in her life, something which was driving her every action. She did acknowledge to herself that George had become important as well, but she reasoned that finding Harry and being with George were two sides of the same coin.

She decided she needed to write to George to update him on what had happened, although she was disappointed with the reply from him to her last letter. He did not mention Harry or the sightings that she wrote to him about. He told her a little about what life was like for him there, intimating that he missed her and was fond of her, asking about family and friends. But nothing about Harry. She thought it was because he did not want to encourage her.

That was true.

George did want her to stop her, as he saw it, misguided campaign, to find Harry. But there was more. It was as if he was afraid of even writing Harry's name. That it would bring back the thoughts and dreams again. But it was too late. The conscious thought that he should not include Harry in his reply to Ada was enough to make George agitated, unsettled again. To make him feel sick. The anxiousness was back in full force.

After another day grooming and feeding the horses, George and Ali were sitting on bales of hay in the stables.

"Yes, Egypt for the Egyptians, but that is not enough. That is only the beginning. Look at what is happening in Sudan." George had wanted to know what Ali thought about the recent troubles in Egypt. If he had joined in the demonstrations and chanting. Ali waved that aside.

"It doesn't matter about what is happening here. In Sudan something more important is happening."

"Why? What?"

"The Sudanese, the Dervish and the Ansar people are casting aside Turkish and Egyptian rule. But it is the reasons why that are so important. Yes, the Sudanese are taxed within an inch of their lives, and they are beaten up by the Bashi-Bazous if they can't pay. But there is a more important reason why they want to free themselves."

Ali paused to give what he had to say next a more dramatic impact.

"It's about who we are. Our beliefs, our religion. It is the threat to our very souls that has caused the black flag to be hoisted in Sudan."

"Black flag...?"

Ali ignored George's interruption. "Islam is not the religion of princesses or Muftis, or high Western-style living, or corrupt money-making officials." He was no longer looking or sounding like the mischievous stable boy. His voice had become earnest, his face was stern, his eyes wide. He leaned towards George, his right hand was a fist that gestured up and down with each word.

"It is not the religion of the rich who pay lip service to the words of the Quran, such as the Turks and Egyptian rulers, while the masses are poor and sometimes starve. Islam, as taught by Muhammad (peace be upon him) is the religion of the poor and of the many. It is a revolutionary religion." Ali stopped for a moment. He could see that George was taken aback. So, he relaxed his body, leaned back, and in a quieter, lighter voice he continued.

"You see, in Sudan the word is taught by mystics, by local elders, shamans. Teachers who travel the country and who are fed and maintained by each village they visit, or who set up a temple to which people come and listen and learn. They teach a pure, untainted way of life and belief, one that they themselves follow. Not the bastardised and corrupt version imposed by the Turkish state."

It was a lot for George to take in. But he picked up on one thing. "You said it's about who we are. But you're an Egyptian, not a Sudanese chap."

Ali ignored him.

"The revolution in Sudan is being led by the son of a carpenter, and you know how propitious that is," he said. George didn't know what, 'propitious' meant, but he worked out from what he was saying that it was probably something good.

"'You mean like Jesus?" George said.

"Yes. This man is called Muhammad Ahmad Ibn Abdallah. He is the son of a boat builder in Dongola on the banks of the Nile. His father traces his line from the prophet Mohamed so you can imagine how important Muhammad felt he was, even from an early age."

"How did he get from being a boat builder to stirring up all this trouble?"

"He was never really a boat builder. He told his father that he wasn't cut out for it."

Ali spoke in another, higher, child-like voice, acting the part of Muhammad.

"Father. My hands are too soft for this trade. I have another calling, a spiritual calling. Cutting down trees and hewing logs into hulls is not why I am here."

Ali then reverted to his normal voice.

"His father came to a decision which has had consequences, perhaps for us all. While he was still expected to cut down the trees and hew the logs, he was also sent to a Khalwas,"

George gave a puzzled shrug.

"It's a special Islamic school. The discipline is strict. The students are expected, through chanting and repeating and endlessly copying the Quran, to learn it by heart."

It reminded George of the endless chanting of numbers and letters at the national school he went to before going to Mrs Clatworthy's.

Ali suddenly let out a scream of pain and shook his hand. He looked at George's shocked face and laughed. "That's what it's like in a Khalwas. If you don't concentrate, you get struck on the knuckles with a stick. Little Muhammad was never struck, he always concentrated. And he learned. He learned to hate the Turks and the Egyptians – for him and his teachers, they have been guilty of apostasy."

Again, Ali could see that George was lost. "It means they were aware of the true faith but turned their back on it. They have copied the customs and lifestyles of Christians and Jews and diluted their Islamic faith. This is worse than being an infidel who has never known the true way."

"What do you think, Ali?" asked George. "Do you agree with this. Do you think the Turks and Egyptians are, you know, what you said?"

Ali looked around to see if anyone was near, "You said to me just now that I was Egyptian, not Sudanese. But there is something more important than these made-up descriptions of who we are. Yes, I am Egyptian, but, more importantly, I am a follower of the true faith. I have more in common with my brothers in Sudan than the corrupt sultans and kings here. Yes, they should throw off the yoke of the foreign rulers, and we should do the same here and with them create a new caliphate. Perhaps the Mahdi will do this."

"The who?" George asked.

"The Mahdi. Muhammad proclaimed himself the Mahdi two years ago. Mahdi is the expected one, the right guided one, the one to lead the faithful to the true faith."

"What about us? The British?"

"You? You should leave, go home. This is not your land, you are infidels. If you do not go, then you will die."

"Is that what you think? I thought we were friends?"

"Yes, we are, but my faith is more important than friendship, or even my wife and children. I must die for it, or you and your people must die. We cannot both exist in this place."

Ali could see that George was shaken by this remark. "We can be friends," he laughed, "and perhaps this can end without bloodshed after all." Ali then looked around. "I must get back to the horses before the sergeant major gives me a hiding!" He laughed again, jumped up and walked briskly back to the stables.

"George!" It was his corporal who came walking over to where he was sat. "Bloody awful news. Seems a column sent by the Egyptians to sort out Sudan has been wiped out. It was led by an Englishman called Hicks, he's been killed as well. Shouldn't be surprised if we see action over this.'"

George nodded and looked over his shoulder at Ali who was now putting down fresh hay in one of the stables.

The 3rd Battalion, Kings Royal Rifle Company remained in Alexandria, Egypt, without further explanation from its officers. The Company had commandeered a building near to their camp which they called the 'spit and polish.' It was provided with some beer and rum and turned into a sort of 'other ranks' club. After all, they thought, the officers have posh clubs in the city – why not us as well.

George and a few of his friends were sitting in the club one evening after duties were completed when, without prompting one of them stood up, opened his arms to the rest of the room and began a recitation:

Just a week or two ago my dear old Uncle Bill,
He went and kicked the bucket and he left me in his will.

He had a good voice. He knew how to perform. He had all the gestures and the expressions. He could have been on the stage of a music hall.

So, I went around the road to see my Auntie Jane.
She said, "Your Uncle Bill has left you a watch and chain."

Everyone in the room was laughing and drinking. It was like being back home. Down the pub having a sing song.

Except it wasn't home. It was hot, and there was a feeling of uncertainty among the men.

So, I put it across my derby Knell.
The sun was shining on it, and it made me look a swell.
I went strolling round about.
A crowd of kiddies followed me and they began to shout:

He raised his arms towards the room, and everyone joined in:

Any old iron? Any old iron? Any, any, any old iron?
You look neat. Talk about a treat!
You look so dapper from your napper to your feet.
Dressed in style, brand new tile,
And your fathers old green tie on.
But I wouldn't give you tuppence for your old watch and chain,
Old iron, old iron.

They enjoyed trying out the new songs from the London music halls. They had all just taken in a deep breath to belt out the next verse when they were interrupted by a sergeant major who came smartly in, swagger stick under his arm.

"All right lads. Another hour then time for kip. You need to be up ready for full kit inspection at 0600 hours."

They groaned.

"'Now now lads. We are off on a lovely little boat trip."

6

Trinkitat

It was the last thing the British Government wanted, another costly military adventure. This was not the way things were done. The British used their power, prestige and wealth to achieve their political and imperial aims by proxy. Its huge powerful and modern navy ruled the world's seas, but its small, albeit highly professional and well-equipped army, was to be used only when absolutely necessary. There was to be no Crimea debacles again.

The recent invasion of Egypt had been swift and successful. But – even so, another expedition so soon? It looked as though there was no choice.

With history repeating itself as a farce, as a tragic farce, the Turkish/Egyptian Government had decided to send another expedition into Sudan to quell the revolt. Like the Hicks' column it was underprepared and again led by a British Officer, Valentine Baker, a man without a distinguished service record. A man who was cashiered from the British Army for attempting to assault a young girl on a train.

Once again, the force was almost destroyed by Sudanese rebels under the command of Osman Dinga, one of the Mahdi's most senior officers. Baker and a few others escaped by the skin of their teeth.

There were British and other Europeans across the Sudan, particularly Khartoum where the Ascetic Celibate Christian General Gordon led a crusade to rid the area of slavery. Another cause of the Mahdi-led revolt in the region.

Reluctantly, the British government stirred. There was no desire to commit to yet another costly invasion of what was considered a worthless lump of North Africa. Even amongst Muslims Sudan was a joke. The saying was that after Allah had created Sudan he laughed. Nevertheless, it was recognised that something should be done to help Britons and Europeans flee from the clutches of the Islamic uprising. A British army expedition would be sent to defeat and destroy Osman Dinga's forces, and in turn crush the momentum of the revolt and the morale of the insurgents. While the Mahdi and his Dervish hordes licked their wounds, the evacuation could take place. But the expedition was to do no more. Once it had achieved its aim, it was to leave Sudan.

In Alexandria and after three false early morning starts, each of which included a full kit inspection, George, and his company, were once again boarding an ironclad. Next day they had anchored by the small Red Sea port of Trinkitat on the Sudanese coast.

The ship they were on was too big to moor alongside the flimsy-looking wooden jetty, so large, flat-bottom lighter boats transported the men and horses and other equipment to the shore. The sea was a little choppy and George, almost mesmerised, stared at it as the craft butted its way towards land. "Too rough to skim," he said to himself.

"What?" Asked another in the boat.

George shook his head. "Nothing."

The army assembling on the coast over the next few days included a number of different brigades, all, in the view of George and his comrades, "Top notch."

There was his own battalion, the 3rd Kings Royal Rifle Company, considered the best mounted infantry in the British army. The cavalry was the 10th and 11th Hussars, the infantry consisted of battalions from the Black Watch, Gordon Highlanders, Irish Fusiliers, the Yorks and Lancs and Royal Marines. There was also a Royal Artillery company and a company of Royal Engineers. All in all, there was about 4,500 men ready to move against Osman Dinga.

The expedition was commanded by General Sir Gerald Graham, also known as Gee Gee, but not in his hearing. Graham was in his early fifties. Tall, good looking with a mane of hair and a luxurious moustache, he was known as a brave and aggressive commander. Indeed, he had won the VC as a Lieutenant in the Crimea leading a ladder party at the assault of Sebastopol. He was born in Acton where George and his family lived for a while, but Sir Gerald lived in quite a different neighbourhood.

Despite the size of the expedition being assembled, all the men involved knew the Dervish and Ansar army was likely to be bigger, much bigger. But they told themselves, they had discipline, superior weapons and they were British. But as they set up camp and made sure the horses were comfortable, stories circulated among them about the screaming, spear-throwing, sword-wielding tribesmen they had come to call the 'fuzzy wuzzies.'

"They sound bloody terrifying," said one soldier as they all sat down to drink mugs of tea during a break.

"Yeh, and they've got hold of artillery from that massacred Hicks expedition and the one led by that toff Baker," said another.

"I was told that Baker is here."

"What? Here in the camp?" Asked George.

"Yeh. Seems Sir Gerald thinks he would be useful as he knows the area."

"He got his arse kicked though, didn't he? Lost a load of his men."

George's corporal joined the sitting men as they talked about Baker. "He tried to have his way with a girl on a train," he said. They stopped talking and looked at the corporal. "Yeh, it seems she climbed out of the carriage door and held on to the outside she was so terrified."

There were gasps and a few mutterings of, "Bloody hell" and, "Would you believe it".

The corporal went on. "He went to the nick for a year and then was chucked out of the army. But here he is 'advising' our commander."

"So, he is here?"

The corporal nodded.

"ATTENTION!"

It was the day after they had landed, and the men were ordered to parade for inspection. Word had got around that one of the inspecting officers would be Baker. Sure enough, among the inspection group was a man in a blue Turkish uniform, bedecked with medals and a red fez on his head. He was large and full faced, with a droopy moustache and brooding eyes, walking slightly stooped and round shouldered, with his hands clenched behind his back.

In the back ranks there was mumbling. George, nearer the front, knew what it was about.

"PRESENT ARMS!"

The men were unhappy at being inspected by a man who was thrown out of the British army. Particularly given the reasons he was cashiered.

"This bloke's bad luck," hissed someone behind George, as the inspection group passed by. "What's he doing back with the British army?"

"ORDER ARMS!"

"I heard that a lot of our officers feel the same," whispered another. "But it seems Sir Gerald thought his local knowledge would be useful."

"Well, it wasn't useful when he got smashed up by Dinga, so why would it be now?" Came the reply. "Seems wrong a bloke like that lording it over us."

Baker walked past the ranks looking forward and downward, but not at them. For the men it was an indication of shame. For Baker, he did not care. It was the way he always walked. Round shouldered, mouth curved downward, framed by a similarly shaped moustache. The men were of no concern to him.

The day after the parade and inspection, George's corporal asked him to join him on a scouting trip around the area. The aim was to have a look at the ground they will be crossing over soon, and whether there were any barriers or obstacles that might get in the way.

Under a blazing sun they trotted across a barren, undulating landscape of scrub. The monotony was broken here and there with a few grasses and scatterings of bitter apple pods. In the distance they could see a blue haze of mountains, then after another half an hour of riding, a line of small Cyprus trees. As they came closer, they could see the trees stood on the bank of a narrow riverbed. It was largely dry but there was a thin, turgid flow of water in the middle of it.

"Hardly your Thames, is it?" The corporal said to George.

"No corp."

They followed the river and soon saw a group of figures ahead of them. George's sharp eyes were able to confirm that they were 'our blokes.' As they got nearer a guard who had been watching them waved.

"All right mates?" he called. "What lot are you?"

"Kings Royal," said the corporal. "You?"

"Royals Engineers. Putting a pontoon bridge over the river. Having a break for a bit. Fancy a brew?"

"Thanks, but we've got to get on," the corporal answered.

The Engineers were sitting down resting and chatting together. George and the corporal exchanged nods and greetings as they trotted by. One of them was sitting with his back to a rock and a little away from the others. He had taken his solar topee off and was looking out at the empty landscape, seemingly lost in thought. George slowed down as he neared him. He did not look around. The corporal had not noticed and kept going.

George looked at the lone Engineer. His eyes, his brow, a thin nose, straight mouth, rounded shoulders. He stopped a few feet from him. The man slowly turned his head and looked up.

George gasped. He tightened his grip on the reins of the horse. His heart thumped against his chest.

The engineer looked at George, nodded and smiled.

"George!"

It was the corporal.

"Come on lad stop idling about."

George spurred his horse and caught up with the corporal.

"What's the matter lad, you look like you've seen a ghost?"

George looked back. The Engineer was still looking towards him. He thought, this was Ada's fault. He was going to see Harry everywhere now, at least people he thought looked like him.

"Sorry corp," he said, and they rode on, but George felt more and more that he needed to talk to someone about Harry. He felt he needed to get some things off his chest about him. But he could not think further than that. He could not sort out the words in his head about it, or the feelings he kept having that filled up his chest and made him gasp for breath sometimes.

7

El Teb

Just a few days after the landing at Trinkikat, on 27th February, the British moved out of their camp and began the march to El Teb, Osman Dinga's base and the place where Valentine Baker's expedition was destroyed. Sir Gerald Grahame's aim was to strike quickly and decisively at Dinga so that evacuations could then take place, then leave Sudan as quickly as possible. He knew that the British Government were trying to persuade the Khedive in Cairo to abandon Sudan. "Leave it to the Mahdi chappie, it's not worth fighting for." But here was Sir Gerald about to do that very thing. Fight the Mahdi or least the Mahdi's proxy, Dinga.

The KRRC battalion was ordered to move ahead of the main force and act as a scouting screen. George was glad to be moving, even though the prospect of a battle was unnerving. At least they were no longer sitting in yet another fly-infested camp, constantly cleaning equipment and drilling.

The infantry marched in column a few miles behind George and his company and behind them was the cavalry with the rest of the mounted infantry. The ground they moved over was the usual scrub and stones and sand, but now, appearing overnight, they could see outcrops of tight bunches of red flowers which ran on tendrils along the ground. They stood out like clots of blood on the bleak landscape.

As they rode ahead, they could hear the main body of men behind. The combination of marching, of wagons and artillery being hauled, of horses clattering and bagpipes made a sound like distant crashing waves.

In less than two days they neared El Teb. It was Friday the 29th of February. George's corporal tried to make a joke about how glad he was that this didn't happen every year, but they were too tense to respond.

Sir Gerald deployed the classic British army formation. The square. A mobile square of infantry which ground forward, followed by the cavalry and George's mounted infantry battalion. As they drew nearer to the Dervish fortress, George and his company were ordered to ride forward. "Have a look at the enemy positions lads. Size them up for us."

George could feel his heart beating quickly as he rode forward with the others. Within less than a mile they came in sight of a small hill. They halted. An officer observed the hill through his binoculars. It was silent apart from the snorting of the horses. As George looked to his front, he began to make out barricades of wood and rocks and could see figures behind them. Then he realised that the stones and boulders in the foreground were the heads of people looking at the troops from pits and trenches.

He was near the officer with the field glasses who spoke

over his shoulder to a sergeant. "Thousands in the front and second lines and many more behind in reserve. We are outnumbered sergeant. Also, artillery at either end of the trench formation."

"Probably the Krupps guns nicked from the Egyptians sir," the sergeant replied. "I don't expect they know how they work."

"Oh, but they do. Plenty of Egyptian deserters have joined them. They will know how to handle them alright."

The officer looked around at the company. "Right lads fire off a few rounds at the fuzzies. Let's see what they do."

For the first time in his life George raised his rifle to fire at men. People. Humans like him. But he did not have time to reflect on this momentous moment because immediately there was a crackle of gun fire coming from the Dervish positions.

The men around George cursed and swore as their mounts shifted in response to the noise. George muttered, "Fucking hell" to himself. The shots went over their heads. The men knew that this meant the Dervish were untrained in rifle firing, that they had not been taught to adjust the rear sights of their guns to allow for distance. For the Battalion, and indeed all the infantry in the British army, firing smoothly, quickly, and accurately was second nature. They had been drilled, day in, day out, on the techniques of musketry. They had been indoctrinated with the need to remain steady and calm when firing. To trust themselves. To trust their comrades. To mercilessly kill their enemies.

Firing while mounted on a horse was an extra challenge but keeping the horse calm, while keeping yourself calm, was an attribute the KRRC was renowned for. They were told to fire. George aimed in the direction of the Dervish positions. Steadied the horse with his knees. Held his breath to minimise movement, smoothly pulled the trigger, no jerking, no panic shooting, and loosed off a round. The recoil from the Martini-Henry required him to reset himself, the horse, and the gun, but he did this in seconds. Loaded, aimed, held his breath, fired again.

It was too far away to tell what effect their firing was having, but they were quickly told to fall back as the main infantry square had now arrived and was moving forward.

They were ordered to ride to a rise on the left flank of the infantry square. From there George and his company had a panoramic view of the battlefield. At least for a while. They could see the front ranks of the British square discharging disciplined volley fire at the enemy positions. In response the shooting from the Dervish appeared to be sporadic and ill directed. Their artillery fired as well but from what George could see, to little effect. Then the British artillery replied and started to hit Dervish positions. Stone and earthworks exploded. Bodies flew into the air.

There were screams, shouts, a high pitch ululating sound, bagpipes, the thunder of artillery, the rattle of repeating guns, and the deafening explosions of volley fire. George looked on. He felt strangely detached from the action taking place in front of him, as if he was watching an exercise in military manoeuvres. As if it was a show, like the Wild West shows he had heard of with gunfights between cowboys and Indians but where no one was hurt.

But then, as the British front line neared the enemy

trench, George could see tribesmen jumping up and charging with spears and long knives. He could not help but think how brave those men were. The Dervish charge was met with a bayonet charge by the British which halted them.

Someone near George shouted, "There go the cavalry!" Sure enough, they could see the Hussars sweeping towards the Dervish lines.

The Hussars, sabres drawn, thundered forward. They were the battering ram of the British army. Or in keeping with the industrial age, a huge, killing steam roller. Many tribesmen ran as the Hussars approached. Some tried to stand but were hacked down. Some fell to the ground and after the horsemen had passed rose up to try and slit the hamstrings of the horses. But these attempts were in vain. The cavalry had driven off a large part of the right flank of the Dervish army and now returned to its lines.

The battlefield became covered in smoke from the rifle and artillery fire, but through the fog George could glimpse lines of infantry in Khaki with white solar toupees, advancing steadily, bayonets drawn. Sometimes they stood, presenting their rifles and firing, and sometimes fighting hand to hand with the Dervish who were rushing at them with spears. The sounds rolled around this once-empty land, now filled with men in a desperate and bloody struggle.

They watched, lined up on that little hill, in silence apart from little chats to the horses and pats to keep them calm and under control.

They were tense. George knew his company could be called into action at any moment. His corporal knew how his men felt because that is how he felt. So, it was time to say something to keep them calm and in control. Over the clamour and noise of the battle he called down the line, "Remember lads, you're fighting for Queen and country, but mostly you are fighting for your mates. Right lads?"

They shouted back, "Right corp!"

"You wouldn't let your mates down, would you?" he shouted again.

They replied loudly, "No corp!"

George looked down the line of his comrades. Like him, they were keeping their horses in check as the waves of hot noise and metal, and explosions and blasts and screams swept around them. The air was full of stray bullets passing with a zing or a forlorn whine.

He looked at his mates in line either side of him and thought, "Will I let you down, will I let you down?"

Amongst all that din, George fell into a sort of daydream. But his 'dream' was not an escape from the fear and apprehension. Instead, it was vivid and shocking. Sitting on his horse he felt his arse getting wet and warm.

Harry is sitting on the hard cold wooden floor right next to me. We are squashed in, we are touching. Harry's thin warm body touching me. Then the water trickled and then flowed and began to seep into Harry's ragged shorts.

Harry looked down, and then at me.

"What have you d…done," he said quietly.

"Don't tell." Then I shouted, "Miss! Harry's wet himself!"

I did not look at him, but I could hear Harry choking on his words, unable to say anything in his defence as Mrs Clatworthy waded towards him. If she had looked properly, she would have seen it was not him who caused the wetness. But it would not have been the first time, so she laid into him. In his heavy wet shorts, Harry was expelled into the freezing cold while I cosseted as the innocent victim, was led in front of the blazing fire to dry out.

"Fuck me!"

George was shocked. Who would have dared say that with Mrs Clatworthy in the parlour?

"That was bloody close," It was a trooper near him spurring his horse back into line.

"All right Alf?" Someone asked.

"Bullet nearly took my bleeding hat off!" he replied.

George was back on the little hill, back in the noise and the shouts. He looked at them. His mates. The ones he would never let down. But now he was not so sure, because now he was different. His account of that time in Mrs Clatworthy's parlour had suddenly changed after so many years and repeating it so many times in his head. He had always felt bad about telling on Harry, but now the story he had told himself was worse than a betrayal, bad as that was. It was a cowardly act.

George did something bad, but Harry got the blame, and it was Harry who was punished while George was consoled. And then the feeling he had then, came back. The feeling that he was relieved that nothing bad had happened to him, and remembering that feeling, that cowardly feeling, made him feel sick.

He was suddenly aware of Suzy, his horse, starting to get frisky as more loose shots whizzed around their heads and the noise of the battle became even louder. An officer rode up in a hurry to the company and shouted to the sergeant.

"Get your lads down there." He pointed to where infantry men were engaging tribesman who were taking cover behind rocks and barricades at the near end of the battlefield, "And support the infantry in driving those bastards off."

The order was given to make ready. They unholstered their Martini-Henry's, loaded them and carrying them at their side, with one hand on the reins, started to gallop in line down the little hill.

George repeated under his breath, again and again as he rode forward, that he would not let his friends down. More bullets whizzed around and over them. The screams and the noise became louder. They knew they would have to dismount and fight alongside the infantry when they got down the hill. It meant fixing their bayonets, and they knew it meant they might have to skewer a man or get skewered themselves. George's breath came in short gasps has he rode down towards the battlefield. He wanted to defecate. In fact, he thought he would there and then on Suzy, but by the time they got down the hill he felt better. The pressure in his stomach had relented.

The tribesmen were running, the cavalry chasing after them again and cutting more of them down. There were Dervish bodies lying all over the ground, some still moving and groaning.

It was over. George and his company had hardly fired a shot. Did not need to dismount and fix their bayonets and skewer a person. But what they saw was horrible, and George was relieved that nothing bad happened to him and that he did not shit himself.

Over two thousand Dervish were killed against just a handful of British soldiers, with some fifty-odd wounded, including Valentine Baker who got a bullet in the jaw. When they found out, someone in George's company said, "That'll shut him up."

They spent the night camped near the village of El Teb. Everyone was talking about the battle, full of themselves. Everyone had a story to tell about the day or were able to add something to someone else's story. George did too, although the experience of his company was nothing compared to the bloody and personal horror of the infantry. But even as he was joining in with the recollections of the day, and the almost hysterical laughter that followed each story, laughter betraying the relief of being alive and in one piece, of being in a battle and not running, even as he was joining in, he could not forget what he had remembered.

He could not leave it alone. As they sat around the fire talking, laughing, pushing each other playfully, he could not stop thinking about the person that had emerged from inside him. The person he had avoided all these years. He felt that his head would burn with it. He could not stay where he was, but it was no good going anywhere else because it was inside of him. He could not leave it somewhere and walk away from it. He pretended to eat supper. He held a fixed smile. He didn't want anyone asking him if he was sick.

After a while, the conversation became quieter, the laughter more measured, when a voice like an angel silenced all chat in the camp.

Here's forty shillings on the drum
For those who volunteer to come,

El Teb

To 'list and fight the foe today
Over the hills and far away
O'er the hills and o'er the main
Through Flanders, Portugal and Spain
Queen Vicky commands and we obey
Over the hills and far away
When duty calls me I must go
To stand and face another foe
But part of me will always stray
Over the hills and far away

Now some of the men joined in the chorus

O'er the hills and o'er the main
Through Flanders, Portugal and Spain
Queen Vicky commands and we obey
Over the hills and far away

Then quiet again for the singer with the voice like an angel to sing the verse.

If I should fall to rise no more
As many comrades did before
Then ask the fifes and drums to play
Over the hills and far away

Now all of them in that part of the camp joined the chorus.

O'er the hills and o'er the main
Through Flanders, Portugal and Spain

Queen Vicky commands and we obey
Over the hills and far away
Again, it went quiet for the singer.
Then fall in lads behind the drum
With colours blazing like the sun
Along the road to come what may
Over the hills and far away.

They knew it was the last chorus, men who had been resting on the ground sat up. Others who had been sitting stood up. A mate of George's next to him put his arm around his shoulders and they all sang together.

O'er the hills and o'er the main
Through Flanders, Portugal and Spain
Queen Vicky commands and we obey
Over the hills and far away.

A moment's silence was followed by clapping and calls of "Well done mate!" and "That were good." Then quiet, then a call from further away. "Officer wants to know who that was singing."

"It was Evans, B Company," someone shouted back.

A moment passed and the voice called back, "Officer says – beautiful."

George sang with the others and singing and listening to the man with a voice like an angel had calmed him. But in the silence that followed, as they bedded down, it all came back, and he choked as he thought how far away those days, before his betrayal and cowardice, were. Those days when he thought he was a good person.

8

Rosey

Although Ada had second thoughts about her search for Harry after the matter with the letter, she decided on one last try to find him. This time though, she would not do it by running around and stirring everyone up.

She decided she would find Harry's older sister Rosey. She felt sure that Harry would have been in touch with her as they were close. This was to be her last throw of the dice.

She went to see Harry's Mum and asked her where Rosey was in service. Mrs Tompkins asked why. "Just wanted to see her again, have a bit of a chinwag," Ada said. She thought better of telling her the real reason for fear it would upset her again given how she reacted to the letter.

Mrs Tompkins looked suspicious. "I didn't know you two got on. What with Rosey being older and all."

Ada was surprised that Mrs Tompkins seemed so reluctant to tell her anything, given how much she looked to Ada for help over Harry. She thought of simply telling Mrs Tompkins the real reason, that Rosey might know where Harry is. But something prevented her, and now it was not because she was concerned it would upset her. Mrs Tompkins response had put Ada on her guard. Now she decided that it would be better that Mrs Tompkins did not know her reasons, so she said, "Not that much older and yeh, we used to have a chat about this and that when we would meet." This was not true, but Ada was determined to follow through with her plan. Even if it meant making things up to achieve it.

Rosey's mum said nothing. So, Ada asked, "How often does she come home?"

"Never been home since she left," came the reply.

The silence that followed became awkward. Ada decided to break it by being forthright. "Anyway. I want to see her so can you tell me where she is working?"

For a moment she thought Mrs Tompkins was going to refuse, thought she was going to tell her to go. But no. She went to a dusty, crumbling wooden fire surround and on the mantelpiece took a piece of card from behind a candle holder. "You'll have to remember it, it's all I got."

Ada could see she was in service in Reigate, Surrey, which was a bit of a trip. She said the address to herself, "The Lodge, Reigate Heath."

"I'll write to her and see when I can call on her."

Mrs Tompkins snorted, "You can write if you like, but she can't read."

Ada had had enough of Mrs Tompkins and her surly attitude. She said quickly, "Well I'll get the train and take my chances then." She then went to the door. "Goodbye."

Mrs Tompkins stood and watched her leave and said nothing. As Rosey walked away, she became sure that Mrs

Tompkins knew exactly why she wanted to see Rosey, and clearly did not like the idea.

Sunday was her usual day off from the milliners and Ada decided to use her next one to visit Rosey. All that week she wondered if she would find Rosey and if she did what she would have to say. But she also could not get out of her head how Mrs Tompkins was towards her. Why would she be so difficult, so, well, almost aggressive?

The next Sunday Ada got up early and walked to Brentford station, got a return ticket to Reigate and was told where she had to change. Also, that it being Sunday, there would be a bit more waiting. She got out first at Kew Bridge and waited forty-five minutes for the next train to Clapham Junction where, after another half an hour wait, she got the train to Reigate.

She had copied the address down on a piece of paper which she showed the porter at Reigate station. "The Lodge, Reigate Heath," he read from the card. "Yeh, it's a bit of a walk love, but if you go out of here, straight down the high street, then as you come out the other side, the Heath is up on your left. You'll see some big houses there. It's one of them."

It was about midday by the time Ada set off from Reigate station, and it was warm and sunny. At the end of the High Street there was a pub opposite a sizeable pond with swans and ducks. Sitting by the pond was a small figure in a faded-red cape with the hood up. Next to the figure was a perambulator. The figure was motionless. Ada was intrigued by this slight, still person just staring at the fowl on the pond. She slowed her walk to try and catch a glimpse of the face hidden by the hood. The figure moved a little, hearing the footsteps, and Ada saw the profile. She caught her breath. It was Harry.

No, of course it wasn't, she told herself. It was Rosey.

"Rosey?" Ada called and slowly walked towards the figure. Rosey started, and turned around, confused. She shielded her eyes and looked at Ada walking towards her. "Ada Marlow?" She said, "What are you doing here?"

"Looking for you."

As Ada drew closer, she could see that Rosey, a narrow-faced, sharp-featured young woman, looked even thinner and more angular than when she last saw her. Indeed, Rosey looked pale and sickly. Her eyes were big and wide in her pinched, bony face.

Looking both anxious and angry, Rosey blurted, "Did my Mum send you?"

"No, Rosey."

Rosey's face and body relaxed a little, "That's all right then."

Ada decided to talk about the baby as she could see that Rosey was agitated. "Lovely little bundle. Boy or girl?" she asked.

"Boy."

"Looking after him then, for someone in the house?" Rosey didn't answer. Ada thought the perambulator looked a bit old and rusty for someone posh enough to live in a big house.

As if in a trance, Rosey slowly looked away from Ada, and went back to staring at the swans and ducks on the pond.

Feeling awkward, Ada asked if Rosey minded her sitting on the grass nearby. Without taking her eyes off the pond Rosey gave a resigned shrug.

There was a long pause filled by birdsong and ducks chattering to each other. It was clear that Rosey was not going to instigate any conversation, so Ada decided to get to the point of her visit.

"Look Rosey, I've been trying to find Harry…"

Before she could continue Rosey shot her a look and said loudly, "Harry has gone!"

"I know," Ada said, "But gone where?"

"Heaven, I hope!" said Rosey and angrily looked back at the pond.

"So, you haven't seen him?"

"How could I?"

There was another long silence. Ada started talking about the baby again, but Rosey interrupted, "You sure my Mum didn't send you?"

"No, she gave me this address, but I came about Harry – it was my idea. I can see it was a waste of time now."

There was another silence filled again by the sound of ducks and other birds.

"It's mine," Rosey said, nodding sideways towards the baby but keeping her eyes on the pond.

"Oh."

"Son of the lady what employs me," she said, staring ahead. "She's been good about it as long as I keep me mouth shut about the father. Kept me on, just bread and board, and a couple of shillings, most would have slung us out, but at least we have a roof."

There was another pause. Then Rosey looked around at Ada and said in a matter-of-fact way, "It's not my first. That was when I was still at home. When I told me Mum about it she called me a whore, but I'm not. I really liked him. The first bloke that is. Not so much him at the house. He said, the first bloke that is, he said we would wed but he buggered off somewhere. Didn't see him again. Dad went wild when he found out. Wilder than he usually does, but he didn't hit me this time. They kept me home. Said to people I was sickly."

Ada remembered something about Rosey not being around a while back. Going down with something or other. At death's door and all that.

It was as if the dam had been breached. Rosey suddenly started to talk quickly. She looked wild. It was as if she was speaking about it for the first time, as if it were a confession she needed to make,

"I had the baby, it wasn't very well, he was sickly. He was only a couple of weeks old. I was out of the room and Mum and Dad were with it. When I came back, they said it had gone."

Rosey's eyes reddened, she swallowed. Ada was about to say something, but Rosey started again, "I grabbed it. It was lifeless, like a little doll. I looked at them and shouted, 'You did this!' They said not to be so daft. They said they would have to hide it as only them knew about it. But, of course, Harry did as well. He told me he was going to tell the police. 'Ere, have you got anything to eat or drink?"

Ada, hanging on every fraught word, was momentarily caught off balance as Rosey shifted from her emotional confession to the request for food.

Ada said she did not but would get something from the pub if she wanted. Rosey nodded. So, Ada went to the pub and bought bread, cheese, and milk.

Back at the pond, Rosey had not moved. Nor, Ada realised, had the baby since she had arrived. No movement, no noise. "Milk for the baby? Mixed with a bit of water?" Ada suggested when she got back.

"No. I'll try myself."

Rosey took the bread and cheese, and the milk. Ada sat by the pond waiting for her to talk again, but also wanting her to pick up the baby, feed the baby, make sure the baby was all right.

After a while Rosey spoke. "I told him not to. Harry. I told him not to tell the police. But a while later, just before I left to go into service Dad was belting him again for something – or nothing, and he got away. He stood in the door and shouted, 'I'm going to tell the police what you did! About what you did to Rosey's little, 'un, and where you put it!'"

"He shouted all this without his stutter. I'll never forget their faces. They looked at each other, then me, all the time Harry was shouting about it. Then Dad jumped towards him, but Harry got away." She took another bite from the bread. "It wasn't long after that when Harry……" She looked at Ada not finishing the sentence.

Ada was glad she was sitting on the grass as she was sure her legs would have gone weak. She came to find Harry, who she was sure was alive. But here was his sister telling her…. well, what exactly was she telling her? It was as if the world had lurched. It was almost physical, like the train this morning crossing over some particularly rough points.

There was silence again. Suddenly the baby started snuffling, and then started to cry. Ada was relieved. In this strange world she had found herself any awful thing started to seem possible. The baby stirring was a welcome interruption. She got up, went over to the pram and gushed over the baby, saying how lovely it was. Overdoing the adoration out of relief.

Rosey did nothing. She was preoccupied with her past.

"Sometimes I'm not sure if I've got it all right," Rosey said. "He was sickly. Sometimes I can see myself in the room with him when he went. It's confusing." She looked at Ada. "Perhaps I did it."

The baby's crying increased, so Rosey got up, went over to the pram next to Ada, and picked the baby up. "Will you come and see me again?" she asked Ada.

Ada said she would, then said goodbye with a kiss on the cheek and left for the station. Looking back, she saw Rosey watching her, standing, holding and rocking the baby. She looked lonely; she looked, thought Ada, like there was nothing for her in this world.

As Ada walked away, she could hear Rosey's thin sad voice singing to the baby.

Lavender's blue, dilly dilly,
Lavender's green
When you are King, dilly dilly,
I shall be Queen

She looked around again, Rosey looked pathetic. But then again, she always did.

On the train home Ada could not stop thinking about the implications of Rosey's story. It made her think again about the reactions of Mrs Tompkinson when she got the letter. Ada now saw it in a different light. Mrs Tompkinson was frightened that Harry was alive, not happy or relieved. Her bursting into tears was just a show. And Rosey's story also explained why Mrs Tompkinson was so hostile when Ada visited her asking for Rosey's address. Mrs Tompkinson was afraid that Rosey would tell Ada what had happened. Well, Rosey did, and Ada now knew. But what did she know, and what could she do about it?

9

Tamai

Gee Gee Grahame was in a hurry. British colonial war doctrine was to keep up the offensive momentum, be always aggressive, never let the enemy regain its balance. This suited Grahame's gung-ho personality down to the ground. He ordered a forced march to the coastal town of Suakin, which was under the control of the Mahdi's forces.

As they prepared to leave their camp, George's company sergeant major explained that although they had given the Dervish a walloping at El Teb, they had not broken up their army, which still numbered ten thousand. So, the job needed finishing.

On the road to Suakin, word came down the line that the Dervish and Ansar had abandoned the town. "Didn't want another kick up the arse," laughed one of George's company.

"Or choosing their ground carefully," said the corporal.

Suakin was not impressive. "I think I would have fucked off from here as well," the company sergeant major said. Patrols were sent into the town and tents were erected outside.

A zariba was constructed around the camp, a defensive wall of acacia thorn, to put off any would-be night-time intruders.

By the campfire that night, the corporal quietly asked George if he was all right.

"Yeh, I'm all right thank you corp," George answered

"Only you don't seem to be the same. You were full of it a few months ago. Life and soul and all that. Wondered if something was up."

"No corp. Nothing wrong. Just tired."

"Only sometimes when lads find themselves in battles, when they see dead people and all, it can upset their heads. Make them think about things."

"I'm not thinking about things corporal…"

"Because if you do feel bad you can always pray with me. You can always reach out to our Lord Jesus."

George had forgotten that the corporal was religious. It reminded him of his dad. Except the corporal had more to say about the world they lived in than Charlie.

"I'll bear that in mind corp."

In truth, George's mind was racing. He started to doubt his recollections again. He began to think that if he was wrong about which of him or Harry pissed himself the first time, then he might be wrong again. Perhaps he didn't even tell Mrs Clatworthy about Harry. Perhaps he just said that he, George, was wet, all innocent like, and she thought it was Harry who done it. He comforted himself that it would be more like him to have said it that way. Then, reassuring himself further, he was sure he never pissed himself as a kiddie, so that it must have been Harry anyway.

Over the next day or so, he began to feel a little better.

Perhaps, he thought, he wasn't the bad person he had come to believe he was. But this mood was fragile. Sometimes, from nowhere, self-doubt and guilt would once again assail him. At night or when he thought too much.

Within a few days the army set off again. They marched for an entire day. It was hot, and the horses were getting bitten by mosquitoes. So were the men for that matter. As before, they were surrounded by endless scrub and sand. Who would want this land, they would ask themselves? Leave them to it, was the consensus.

George's see-saw emotions kept trotting alongside him as he rode with his company. He could not shake off the doubt about himself. As he rode along in the warmth, he started to think that he needed something to prove to himself that he was a good man. He started to think that it would be good to be in another battle and have the chance to take a risk to help his friends. He thought that such an act would clear all the horrible thoughts from his head.

He contemplated death. Would he go as far as to risk death? He fell into a fantasy conversation, first with his mother, but then he switched it to Ada. "It's not that I want to die. I wouldn't try to die. But if I knew I was dying, I would accept it."

He imagined Ada's reply, 'Don't say that.' Yes, that's what she would say. Or would she say, 'Stop talking nonsense, don't try and be some hero.' Yes, she might say that.

Then his thoughts were interrupted.

"So, I said if you haven't got the stuff give me my money back…"

George was confused. It was the rider next to him. He

had been talking to George unaware that George had been talking to Ada, at least in his head.

"What?" George asked.

"No stuff, no money!" The other rider could see that George was perplexed. "Never mind. In a bit of a daydream, were you?"

George nodded.

"Thinking about the little girl back home?"

"No. I haven't got anyone back home."

"Cor blimey. Nothing to look forward to when you get back. That's hard. Anyway, you're still young. I've got a lovely little girl back home. When I get back, I'm gonna…"

George interrupted. He did not want to hear what the other was going to do. And he had changed his mind. He did have a girl back home. He was sure Ada liked him. Perhaps she liked him a lot. And he realised just how much he needed her. "Well, I suppose I have really. A girl back home that is."

The other rider laughed. "Suppose? You need to be more certain chum."

"No. I'm certain. It's someone to live for, isn't it?"

"Suppose so."

George decided to change the subject to one he thought his companion would appreciate, "Let's hope we can have another crack at the fuzzies soon, eh!"

"Blimey, is that what you want? I just hope they fuck off again when they hear we're coming."

A couple of miles from the village of Tamai where the Dervish and Ansar army were, the British expedition camped. Again, they built a zariba of acacia thorn around the tents. After securing the camp the men had their tea, bully beef and hard biscuits, and settled down for the night.

George quickly fell asleep, and he began to dream of a noisy train coming down the tracks, passing by where he was standing. It was making a lot of noise. Then, a loud rasping voice woke him.

"Oi, are you lot bleeding deaf or something?" George struggled to comprehend why he was no longer beside a train track. It was dark, then he saw a match being lit.

"Don't be a dozy arsehole, no lights, we are under bleeding attack. Get your arses out here and get behind cover!"

George shook off his sleep and dreams, he was back in the camp, in the tent, in Africa. The banging noises continued though. They were shots ringing out in the night across the camp. The Dervish were attacking.

It was about one o'clock in the morning. George crawled out of his tent wearing his trousers and a vest, cradling his rifle in his arms. Mingled with the shots were shouts and the sound of alarmed horses. Someone shouted. "Keep down for Christ's sake!"

George crawled towards two other men laying behind some supply boxes and joined them. The ground was freezing cold. Then, between shots, they could hear the Dervish somewhere out there in the night, calling to them. Sometimes shouting in harsh guttural tones, sometimes with smooth, siren-like ones. It seemed to go on and on.

Then George heard his name called.

In a daze he shouted, "Yes?"

One of the men laying near him hissed, "Shut up chum, they'll start aiming in our bleeding direction."

"Must have dozed," George replied.

"How can you fucking doze with this racket going on?" They lay there. Cold to the bone. Tired and afraid. The shooting and calling seemed never ending.

Then, dawn came, and the air changed in minutes from cold to warm, then to hot. The sun blazed down, burning their faces, necks and ears. The shooting slackened off as some of the Dervish decided to move away now daylight was coming. Despite a few shots still whizzing over their heads George and the other men risked moving and crawling into what little shade there was.

On the other side of the camp, in the daylight, artillery men set up two of the nine-pounders and started firing at the scrub, where they knew the Dervish were hiding. At the same time, navy bluecoats erected a Gatling gun and started firing in the same direction. It was not long before the men in the camp saw the Dervish falling back and could at last get up and move. The night action left just one soldier wounded, but the whole camp was exhausted.

As the day grew hotter, so more troops arrived, but they knew they were still outnumbered by the Dervish and Ansar army. But Sir Graham did not mind and told his officers he didn't mind. "We will form into a mobile square, like at El Teb, and squash them with firepower and discipline again. "They will come on in the same old way and we will defeat them in the same old way." He looked pleased that he was able to turn to a quote from the Duke of Wellington. He thought they probably knew it was a quote from the Duke, but he didn't tell them as some of them may not have known and would think it was his own clever remark.

The officers smiled and nodded in agreement. After the briefing one of the officers said to another. "I know Gee Gee doesn't mind how many Dervishes there are, but I do. I want to know just what we are up against."

"Yes, another scouting job for the mounted infantry before we go in and get our feet wet, as it were," said the other.

"Gee Gee won't care. There could be a million of them, and he will still form us up into a square to trundle towards them." The officer aped the General's voice, "Firepower and discipline gentlemen, that's all we need to squash them." The officers laughed. Despite their concern about numbers, they were still supremely confident about the superiority of their troops and their guns.

From where George and his company were positioned, it all looked familiar. The infantry formed into squares again, this time three of them. The cavalry and George's company of mounted infantry behind.

The ground before them was broken and stony and Tamai was hidden by a rocky outcrop in front of them.

The sergeant major galloped up to George's company. "Right lads I have our orders. We're to skirmish forward and find where the fuzzies are lurking. Officer in charge on his way."

The officer arrived and they set off, initially as a column so they could skirt the square on the left flank. As they were passing, they heard the orders shouted to the infantry to begin their forward march, and the groaning stuttering drone of the bagpipes as they were punched into life.

When they had passed the square, the mounted troops fanned out in skirmish formation.

After little more than ten minutes riding they approached the outcrop. As they got closer, they were told to dismount and move forward on foot. Some troopers remained to hold the bridles of the horses. George and his company spread out and cautiously moved forward, rifles at the ready. They were told to scout the Dervish dispositions. Perhaps fire a few shots at any they could find to see if they could make them run.

In front of George, it was clear that the ground came to a ridge and then dropped away out of sight of the men moving forward. They slowed, then were ordered to crawl the final few yards to the ridge so they could look over and beyond.

George was one of the first to stare down into the ravine. "Christ," he uttered to himself.

Below him was an extraordinary sight. It flashed through George's mind that it was like a picture. There, filling the ravine, were thousands of Dervish and Ansar warriors wearing coloured robes with patches of red and blue on them, making them stand out against the dull grey background, like flowers in the desert. The colours seemed to magnify in the full blaze of the sun.

Some of the men had pillars of hair tied up on their heads which made them look tall and fearsome. Some had shields, huge curved swords and spears. Some had rifles they had taken from the Egyptians. There was a rumbling murmur of voices coming from them. George thought it sounded like a crowd waiting for a football match to start back at home.

The men of George's company only had seconds to take this in. Dervish scouts had seen them, and shots hurtled towards them. At the same time the sound of bagpipes and the crunch of marching infantry told them the main force had arrived.

The men lay on the ground, one of them asked the officer if they were to take a few shots at the Dervish as ordered. "Don't be bloody daft," he replied. "Get back to the horses double quick."

They stood and ran, heads down, shots zipping over them. George became aware as he looked up, that the front rank of the nearest British square was marching towards them.

They reached the horses at the same time as hundreds of Dervish and Ansar warriors started to come out of the ravine. As they did, the troops in the front section of the nearby British square started to charge, bayonets drawn. It was the Black Watch, a crack regiment, but the charge had unhinged the square. No one was sure who gave the order to charge, and it was happening without any realisation that there were thousands more of the enemy climbing out of the ravine and joining those already at the top. At El Teb the Dervish army had broken in the face of such charges. But, this time, it was different.

George had reached his horse and mounted it. Quickly looking round, he could see more and more Dervish emerging from the ravine, screaming, howling, running and jumping towards the charging Black Watch. George's company were caught between the two racing tides of men. They crashed into their own infantry. There was confusion, the horses started panicking, they reared up, they bucked and neighed in fear.

Over the clamour and cries George heard someone nearby shout that more Dervish and Ansar were coming either side of the advancing infantry in which they were now hopelessly entangled.

George was trying to control Suzy among the mess of bodies and other horses bumping and pushing into each other. The men of George's company now realised they were being pushed back on a tide of their own men towards the Dervish and the ravine from which they had just retreated.

The advancing Black Watch had detached itself from the rest of the square and the Dervish had got behind and were able to attack them from the rear. They had broken the square. It was the first time such a thing had happened in British military history. A disaster was looming.

George, on his horse, was being pushed backwards. He could see his corporal and other men of his company caught up with the infantry in the same way, and now Dervish warriors were rushing into the tangle of men and horses. George was right in the middle of it.

Above the shouts and screams George could hear a clear, loud voice.

"Right. Move back lads. Slowly. Keep up the fire."

The noise was a furious, frightening cacophony. Shouts, the panicked snorts and squeals of the horses, explosions, shots, and the sound of the bagpipes still playing. It was utter, desperate confusion, but above it again that voice.

"Don't get separated lads. Stay with your pals."

Amongst this mayhem George tried to describe it to himself as if he was telling someone, as if he was telling Ada. It made him feel as if he would survive to tell the tale. But he did not have the words to hold this conversation in those few seconds. Or rather, he had words like fear, screams, blood, blasts, hot metal, cold steel, but they did not add up to the reality of those moments of terror and brutal death.

George and his company were pitched into a nightmare. The horses were being jostled, there was no room to move, the crush was overwhelming. Beneath him he saw tribesman bayoneted or shot at point blank. He saw his own men getting speared, having limbs severed by sword-wielding Dervish.

Then, amongst that whirlwind of hooves, men, rocks, spears, bayonets, Suzy stumbled violently and tipped forward, sending George flying over her neck and head. He summersaulted in the air and came crashing down on his back. The pain seared through his whole body. He could not move. He was sure his back was broken and, surrounded by struggling feet, legs, and arms, that he would meet his end by being impaled with a spear there on the ground.

The awfulness of what was inevitable was replaced by a desire for it to happen quickly. He told himself his back was broken. A spear in the guts would be better than being dragged away as a prisoner. He knew what happened to prisoners. He lay there remembering what he thought of death yesterday. He was surprised at how ready he had suddenly become for it. He wondered what heaven would be like. He tried to remember what Mrs Clatworthy said about the soul. She said the soul was imprisoned in the living body, and only death allowed it to be free. He had no idea what she was talking about then. But now he did. He was ready, or so he thought.

But although people trod on him and tripped over him, no cruel, piercing spear entered him. He realised that they thought he was already gone.

Then the pain started to ease, and he felt movement

coming back to his body. There was a sudden space around him, an eye had appeared in the storm.

He struggled to his knees. He could feel blood running into his eyes making him blink. He felt a gash on his forehead, but otherwise seemed all right. The hand-to-hand fighting had moved in screams, grunts, crashes and bangs, away from him. He had got away with it.

He had got away with it.

No, he had not. There, about twenty yards away, stood a dervish warrior. Through his blinking blood filled eyes George could see that the warrior had seen him. He was tall and was wearing a long black robe. He wore a keffiyeh around his head and across the lower part of his face so that all that could be seen was his dark eyes which now focussed on George. And he held a spear. A long, awful spear.

George, still kneeling, looked frantically around him for a weapon and up at the warrior who began to walk, then jog towards him, spear extended. There was no weapon and no time to do anything to avoid being pierced by the terrible long spear. He had just enough time to contemplate his end, but not enough to do anything about it. He shut his eyes.

He sensed the warrior standing in front of him and felt the tip of the spear pressing against his chest. But nothing more.

Time passed. The noise of the battle continued a little way off. But here, with George kneeling and the warrior standing in front of him holding the spear against his chest, nothing happened. An observer would think it was a posed tableau. That they were carefully positioned subjects being painted by an artist.

George thought that, in a final act of cruelty, the warrior wanted him to open his eyes before he killed him.

Then he heard his name, "George?"

George had no explanation for what was happening or what he heard. So he opened his eyes. The warrior was towering above him, but he had withdrawn the spear and removed the part of the keffiyeh covering his face.

It was Ali. The myriad possibilities, decisions, alternatives and options since the time they were last together at the stables in Alexandra had combined, to bring them both together on that battlefield. And among the thousands of men on that battlefield it was to be Ali who would be George's executioner. Ali had said as much. That there was only one choice between friendship and faith.

"George," Ali said again.

The blood running from the gash on George's forehead had by now flowed in two streams around his nose, soaked his beard and moustache and started to dribble into his mouth, so that his half attempt to speak became a gurgling spitting sound.

Then George saw another figure. Appearing it seemed from nowhere, at almost the exact spot where he first saw Ali, was a British soldier armed with rifle and bayonet. The soldier stepped stealthily towards the unsuspecting Ali who continued to look at George.

"George. It's me Ali."

The soldier came up right behind Ali and winked at George. George spluttered. It was hardly a warning cry. It was more a noise of incomprehension.

The soldier thrust his bayonet into Ali's back between his shoulder blades. Withdrew it and thrust again.

The smile that had begun to grow on Ali's face changed to a look of disappointment. Then his eyes rolled, and he fell forward onto George who caught him and rolled him to the ground beside him.

Ali, the man who said he was willing to die for his god, who said he would not hesitate to kill George if he became an enemy to his faith, hesitated. George who did not like to hear him say such things, who felt sure their friendship would overcome enmity, had also hesitated. He had not warned Ali. He had allowed him to be killed, not for a belief, but for survival. Ali had hesitated because of their friendship. George had not.

George stood up. He looked around at the grisly, smoked-filled, body charred landscape and saw others going about their awful work. For a moment he wished that Ali had not hesitated, that it was he who was lying there with the others, his blood and not Ali's soaking into the filthy sand. He looked at Ali's body, then walked away.

The battle of Tamai had been a near thing. The British dead numbered almost one hundred, with more than another hundred wounded. Far more than at El Teb. But, once again, it was the bodies of the Dervish and Ansar that littered the battlefield. Four thousand of them. The rapid volley fire, the bayonet, the cavalry, the Gatling gun, the artillery and, in the end, the discipline had won another colonial battle for the British. Gee Gee Graham and his officers were satisfied that the Mahdist rebellion had been decisively checked.

However, Osman Dinga was still at large, the Mahdi himself untouched, the vast interior of the Sudan unpenetrated. And in the middle of it, Queen Victoria's favourite, General

Gordon, was holed up in the city of Khartoum. The British, for a moment, had thought about marching Graham's army across the hot and desolate interior to rescue Gordon. But no. They were sure this was not necessary. The defeat of the Mahdists would allow the safe evacuation of Gordon and the Europeans, without the intervention of Graham's force.

George's horse, Suzy, was never found. He was given another. It was nice enough, but it wasn't Suzy. The little army marched back to the coast and sailed away from Sudan, and back to Alexandria. They were paraded in the main square. They were told they had done their job and done it well. They were told there would be medals for what they had done. Two great British victories. The papers back home will be full of it. They will be re-enacting it in the music halls. Someone will write a song about it. They were heroes.

But when it came to heroes, General Gordon's death and the fall of Khartoum would soon upstage the men of Graham's little army. It would be Gordon's heroism, not them, who the music halls celebrated. It was Gordon death who they then lamented, and it was Gordon whose revenge they then demanded.

10

Ferry Lane

In Alexandria, George got drunk with his comrades. As they lurched around arm in arm, he explained to them how barmy it was to think you could have an Arab as a friend. "He was going to kill me!" he shouted at them. They laughed and agreed you can't have an Arab as a friend. "And you can't spend your life moping over a kid you once knew who died, can you?" They agreed, you can't.

In the days leading up to the KRRC leaving Africa for home, George felt better than he had ever felt. He had fought in and survived two battles. He was getting a medal. He was going home, and he was going to see Ada. He hoped something would come of that. And he had, at last, put all those bad thoughts out of his mind.

Two nights before they were to disembark for home, George, and some of his company, drank too much again. He had a disagreement with one of them. The difference was minor. Later no one could remember what it was about. But their voices became raised, and they ignored others telling them, "Come on now lads." They gripped each other's tunics, and glared face to face, but George had the power to throw the other down on the ground. The rest shouted and laughed, George stood and looked down at the man he had toppled.

The man said, "You bugger, George."

With that, George fell on him and grabbed his throat. The others realised that this was no longer a joke. George was swearing, gasping, crying. So was the other man but gasping for air as George's hands tightened around his throat. Two men dragged George off and held him as the other man was slowly helped to his feet.

There was an attempt to make the men shake hands and put it behind them. But the other man, rubbing his throat, said it had gone too far for that, and George, still being held, was simply staring at nothing and no-one and did not even reply. It was agreed that the incident would not be reported to the officers. George broke away from those restraining him and walked off into the dark maze of Alexandria's streets and alleys.

By the morning he had become a deserter.

In those night-time hours, George had walked, had staggered through deserted, darkened, narrow streets, passing growling dogs, sometimes a small, illuminated window, sometimes a shadowy figure. When he looked up, the stars seemed to move in giant circles in the sky, making him sway. He had no destination. He felt nothing. He remembered nothing. He fell. He got up. He collided with a pen of goats. He went on. It became light.

Then someone shouted, "Oi you!"

He was locked in a room, with a pitcher of water which

he drank and drank. He began to examine himself, to wonder who he was, to wonder what he was doing. It was as if he watched himself being taken in front of an officer who asked him to explain his absence from the barracks last night. He listened to his reply. "Got a bit drunk sir." He was told he was lucky the officer was in good spirits because they were all going home tomorrow. That no further punishment would occur, but any further breeches of discipline would result in serious consequences. He was asked if he understood. He heard himself say, "Yes sir." He was then dismissed.

He saw himself walk slowly across the area used for parades to the barracks. As he walked inside voices said, "Here's George!"

"Blimey he looks rough,"

"Had a bit of a night George?"

George remained silent. He lay on his bed. He closed his eyes. He listened to the sounds.

The next day he did his duties. Made sure his horse was winched aboard the ship. Boarded it himself with full kit. Said only what was needed to be said to perform those duties.

After one day at sea George decided all he could do was to try and survive. So he collapsed. He could not get up, he was unable to speak. He was put in the sick bay where the consensus was that he had picked something up in the desert.

In silence, George sailed back to Southampton. He drank water and intermittently tea. He ate sporadically. He kept his eyes closed. He found he could not stop thinking about Ali and, as he did, also Harry. Ali and Harry were together in his mind. As if they knew each other. As if they were lost brothers that he had betrayed.

They said there was no reason he could not walk or talk and that he had something wrong in his head. When they arrived at Southampton he was taken to a hospital where people acted strangely, where people talked to themselves, screamed, threw themselves against the walls. Still George just could not get up, could not walk, or talk.

They pulled him out of his bed and stood him up one on each side and told him to walk. They pushed him forward. When they let go, he fell. They asked him if he was in pain, but he couldn't talk. He could not work out time. He could not work out how long he had been there. He could smell shit. He could recite oranges and lemons. But not out loud.

Then Ada started to visit. And he spoke his first words for a month.

"Don't ask me questions," George pleaded with her. She agreed and they spoke about now and what next, but not of then and what happened.

Soon, George was able to stand up and walk. Then, one day in May 1885, they said he could go.

His six years with the army were up. He was 25 years old and had two medals. He felt like he had emerged from a long sleep, although dreams and sometimes anxiety reminded him that he was not yet cured. In the last days at the hospital one of the orderlies asked him what he was going to do.

"I don't know," George responded. "I'll stay with me mum and dad for a bit. Sort myself out. There is one thing I am going to do though."

"Oh?"

But George did not answer.

Ada came to the hospital when he was released to

travel home with him, though home had changed. While George was away, Eliza and Charlie, with Bill, Jane and Jim, had finally escaped the stink of the river and the gloom of Brentford for the small rural settlement of Harmondsworth in west Middlesex. It was still near the market gardens where Charlie continued to work, but away from the disease and overcrowding of London.

It was not an easy place to get too. George and Ada got the train to Waterloo. For a while they sat next to each other in silence, swaying, and sometimes bouncing on the seat as the train sped along. George had something to say, and he wanted to say it before the journey ended. He looked at Ada who was looking out of the window at the trees and the occasional house and farm that passed by in a blur. He opened his mouth to speak, but Ada looked around at him and said, "I don't like going backwards," and then she resumed watching the countryside go by.

George was momentarily stumped, but then decided to try again. "Ada, I've something to say."

She looked around at him.

"I've been thinking that perhaps you and I… Well, that we could… You can say no if you want… I would understand,"

"Say no to what?" Ada asked.

"Well, that perhaps we could get…," as he spoke a train going the other way roared passed with its whistle screeching. His final words were lost. Ada knew what he was saying. But she pretended she did not.

"What did you say George?"

He was embarrassed. He looked around the crowded carriage, but no one was taking any notice.

"I said perhaps we should..." this time it was their train that let out a piecing whistle and he raised his voice. "Get married!"

But the whistle had abruptly stopped, and his marital proposal had become a loud shout in the carriage. There was laughter. He went crimson. He looked around and everyone was looking at him, smiling at him, nodding at him. He looked at Ada who had stuffed a handkerchief in her mouth and who was desperately trying to remain in control, tears of laughter rolling down her cheeks.

George leaned awkwardly back in the seat, folded his arms and looked at the floor, wishing it would swallow him up.

When Ada finally spoke some minutes later, she did not answer his proposal. Instead, she asked George, "What are you going to do?"

He thought for moment, then whispered, "Get better. Get a job."

She looked at him. She surveyed his face, looked in his eyes. Looked down at his folded arms. She took the arm nearest to her and pulled it towards her, then held his hand between hers.

"All right," she said quietly. "I will marry you if you do what you've said you'll do."

They had now become objects of interest in the carriage, with people continually glancing at them and smiling at them. "I think they are going to get wed," an elderly women said loudly to her companion. There was an appreciative murmur from the other passengers.

At Waterloo, they decided their best option was to get

a train to Ashford near Staines, still some distance from Harmondsworth. It was now mid-afternoon, and George was concerned about Ada getting back to Brentford, but she ignored his worries. "Let's get you home," she said.

At Ashford, they looked for a horse-drawn omnibus, but none were going where they wanted. One of the drivers pointed to a man sitting on an empty dray cart standing in the road nearby. "Alf should be going in that direction," he said. "He'll take you."

Alf was a friendly, white-whiskered, ruddy-faced drayman. "Not going that far," he told them. "I'm picking up some barrels at Heathrow. You could walk across the heath from there. It'll be just a couple of miles, I reckon."

So, they jumped up into the dray and bumped off down the road. Alf occasionally spoke to them about the weather, or to ask who they were visiting, but most of the time they trotted along in the late afternoon sunshine in silence. They smiled at each other. It was as if, for the first time, they had remembered they had agreed to marry. They held hands. They laughed when the cart lurched or bounced as it hit a hole. George wanted this little journey on the cart, in the countryside, in the sun with Ada to go on forever. Eventually though, they stopped. The tiny hamlet of Heathrow was as far as Alf was going. He then pointed to a footpath. "You can see the church tower at Harmondsworth when you get on the heath. Just head towards it. Nothing in the way."

They thanked him and set off. They walked hand in hand, in silence, with only the sound of a gentle breeze and birdsong drifting across the vast empty heath. After an hour they reached Harmondsworth.

They called out as they walked down the short path to a cottage front door. Eliza opened it, reached up and put a hand on each side of George's head and cried.

They sat and talked. At least George, Ada and Eliza sat and talked. Charlie appeared to busy himself, walking through the room now and then with wood in his hand for the fire, or a hammer to repair something. But Eliza called him. "George has something to say."

Charlie stood looking at George. "Ada and I are going to get married Dad," George said with a smile.

Eliza started to cry and was comforted by Ada. Charlie smiled and nodded. "God bless you both," he whispered.

Ada stayed overnight in the little crowded cottage sleeping with Eliza, while Charlie and George shared another bed. Next day, George walked her to where the bus left for Hounslow. She could walk home to Brentford from there. As they walked Ada told George about her meeting with Rosey. "I don't know what to think. It was as if she was saying that Harry's mum and dad…well, like I said I don't know what to think."

George gave no response but walked along, hands in his pockets, staring at the ground. Ada regretted telling him. She knew how even the mention of Harry could upset him.

As they parted, she kissed him on the cheek. George said he would come and see her soon and look for a job as there seemed to be little available where he was.

As the horses pulled the omnibus away George felt empty and, even though he was home, without Ada, he began to have those bad thoughts again. He knew how Harry went into the river. He knew it was no one else.

At night he lay, unable to sleep, overcome with dark

feelings of immense guilt, that he was bad, that he was cowardly. He could not tell Ada these terrible secrets he held inside him, as he was sure it would end things between them. If there was any way he was going to be released from this burden, he told himself, it would be by marrying Ada and trying to live a normal life.

He told his mum that he needed to move back to Brentford or Hounslow to get a job. "You could go back to the market garden son."

"No mum. I need some decent money. I'm going to get married."

"What sort of job?"

George could hardly say it, but after a struggle he muttered, "Rowe's soap factory. They are always looking for people. I'll get a pound a week there."

"But you always said…"

"Yes, I know. I always said I would never work there. But I've no choice now."

He went to the factory in Ferry Lane and was taken on as a soap licker. Ada found him a cheap room in Brentford, and he started in the factory within days.

The factory in Ferry Lane was huge. It had eleven big coppers in which tallow was boiled with other substances to make soap. It was hot and the smell from the melting tallow made George feel sick. His main job was, with long wooden ladles, to pour the hot liquid from the coppers into frames where the impurities would be separated, then what remained was put into soap moulds. The factory specialised in making Blue Mottled soap which the well-to-do would rub themselves with to smell nice. Working there George never smelled nice. Working there, every day, he looked across at Goats Lane Wharf.

One Saturday he went to see the cricket. Middlesex were playing local rivals Surrey at Old Deer Park in Kew. Ada was working, and so should he, but he could not bear the thought of it. So, he paid a penny and went in to watch his favourite game and wondered, for a few minutes, what was being said about him at the soap factory. But then quickly fell into the rhythms and noises of the game. He remembered his own prowess at cricket and thought he could do as well as many of those on the field, although he excepted from this the greats like Bobby Abel, Read and Arthur Littleton. During the lunch break he walked around to the back of the pavilion. A large man with a long moustache wearing a blazer with a badge was sitting on a deckchair smoking a cigar.

"You with the team?" George asked.

The man, without any change from his expression of haughty indifference, looked at George and said, "I'm on the Middlesex committee. Who wants to know?"

After a moment's hesitation George spoke. "I think I'm better than most of your team."

The man smirked. Took a long pull on his cigar, flicked some ash and looked back at George. "Oh you do, do you? Well come back here at close of play and we will see." The man knocked some more ash off his cigar, got up and went into the pavilion.

George could hardly concentrate on the rest of the play. He had heard that professional cricketers can get a pound a match with a bonus if they win. He could be out in the air, playing this beautiful game, and earning a fortune.

He went to the back of the pavilion when play closed but at first could not find the man. People were packing up and leaving. George thought, well that's that then, when he heard a voice.

"Ah, the new WG Grace. So, you have come." It was the man who George had talked to earlier. He turned to someone and said, "Put the wickets up. We have a young man who thinks he can beat you all. It'll amuse me to see how he does."

George felt embarrassed as the others looked at him and groaned. They unpacked a bag and put on hold the drink they were looking forward to in the pub. "Bobby. Have a bowl at the young man here for me, will you?"

George was given some pads, gloves, and a cricket bat. He walked to the wicket with none other than Bobby Abell the Middlesex and England bowler.

"You know it looks easier when you are sat watching than when you are playing," Abell said in a flat bored voice. He was hoping, after a long day in the field, to have a hot bath, but here was a committee member ordering him to bowl at some spectator with delusions of grandeur. Why?

A few players took up fielding positions. Someone stood behind the stumps. Others watched, arms folded, as George took guard. Abell moved in on his run and released a quick sharp ball. George heard his wicket shatter. He looked around at it. It was splayed, flattened. He looked up. He could see people quietly laughing. Abell simply waited for the ball to be returned. "Another?"

"Yes," said George.

Again, another quick ball, but this time George picked up its length and direction and smote it back over the bowler's head. At that moment he felt as if he had driven all the bad things from his head. As if this pure combination of hand and eye co-ordination had exorcised the demons in him. The next ball was shorter. George rocked back on his heels and cut it to the off side. The sniggering had stopped. The onlookers were now watching intently.

Abell bowled again, it was full and straight and went through him before he had time to react. His wickets were again demolished. He looked up. People were wandering away. He was no different. A two-hit wonder with no defence. "You look good when you attack but fucking awful when you try to do anything else," Abell said, and walked away.

That night George played the four balls he had received over and over again in his head. He couldn't sleep. He knew he would have to find some other way to escape the factory.

Most days George worked until six o'clock at the factory and he would then call in on Ada for some tea before walking back to his room. On this one late night, he was walking away from Ada's when he heard someone say his name.

"George."

It was very quiet, almost a whisper. He looked around but could not see anyone.

"Who's there?" He asked.

"Over here," said the voice. It came from a dark shadow hidden from the gas lamps by a high wall. George walked slowly towards the darkness. He was not sure what to expect or who to expect, and he didn't want to get too close. Gradually a shape appeared in the shadows.

It was small and hunched over. "Hello George."

"Who are you?"

"It's Rosey."

George was confused. "Harry's sister Rosey?"

He could see her more clearly now. She was clutching a baby. She was wearing a cape with a hood which she had up.

"Hello Rosey," he said. "I thought you were in service in Surrey."

"No, not anymore," she whispered. "Got chucked out. Got nowhere to stay."

"What about your Mum?" With that Rosie laughed, a hoarse, sickly laugh.

"You want to know what happened to Harry don't you? Ada told me when she visited."

"I know what happened to Harry," George said and looked away from her.

"No, you don't. If you give me five bob I'll tell you."

"I know what happened to Harry," George repeated, this time said in a way that made it clear there was nothing more to say. He thought, she's just going to make something up because she needs a few bob. Poor beggar.

She was going to say something, but George held up his hand. He fished around in his pocket and found some coppers and gave them to her. "That's all I got love," he said. "But why don't you come to Ada's and have some grub. They might be able to put you up for a bit. Come on, come with me."

"Go and ask Ada first," she said. "I'll wait here."

George walked back down the street and got to Ada's. She answered the door and he told her straight away. "Rosey's just down the street with her little 'un and she's got nowhere to stay."

"Well tell her to come here, right now," Ada told him.

George walked back, but Rosey was not there. He called her name and walked about, but she was nowhere to be seen. Ada came down the street. "Where is she?"

"Don't know."

"I said I would go and see her again," Ada sounded upset. "But I didn't."

"Well, you haven't got a lot of time."

"That's no excuse, I said I would see her again. Some friend I am. What did she say?"

George wondered whether to tell her. They had not talked about Harry for a while. He wondered if it would start her off again, and how he would feel knowing now what he knew. "She got the poke from the place she was in service," he said.

"Why?"

"She didn't say, I didn't ask."

They started to walk back to Ada's house. George could not stop himself from telling Ada, "She said she was going to tell me what happened to Harry." As he said it, he wondered why he said it. But he had said it. Ada stopped so quickly that he ended up walking ahead of her.

"What? You need to find her George. Go on, find her now. I knew he would have been in touch with her. She knows where he is."

George was sure that Rosey was trying to achieve what the writer of the letter sent to Harry's Mum was trying to do. Say anything if it meant the chance of getting a few bob. Except in Rosey's case, he could understand why. Just to keep Ada happy he walked around the area a bit more, but there was no sign of Rosey.

Next day, in the stinking hot factory, George was doing his work ladling obnoxious liquids into frames. The obnoxious liquids that would, when processed, clean people and make them smell nice. A fellow he knew came up and offered a pipe. George took it, and out of sight of the charge hands, they took a break. "You knew Harry Tompkins, didn't you?" the man asked.

George was thrown off balance. He swallowed, and said, "Yeh."

"Yeh, thought you did. My brother, a lighterman, fished his sister out the river this morning. Poor bugger. Looks like she threw herself in."

That night at Ada's George sobbed and sobbed. She held his head against her breasts, and she whispered "You'll be alright George. We'll be alright."

George told her that he had asked about the baby and was told no baby was found. He also asked how they were sure it was her. They said someone thought it was her and they fetched her Mum, who recognised her straight away and that her mother said, "Followed her brother I suppose."

That evening, Ada's Mum and Dad were down the pub. Her attention towards George became warm and they kissed, and they caressed, and they lay on the parlour floor, and there, for those moments, George forgot all the terrible things, and was happy.

11

Lion and Tiger

George and Ada were married on July 5th 1885 at St Mary's Church, Harmondsworth. After the marriage, family and friends went to the Five Bells, where a trestle table with food had been set up in the pub yard.

George had beer bought for him. He lost count of how many he drank. Ada told him to stop but he said he was all right and that she should enjoy herself. At some time during the party, he stood on a table and sang;

There's a tavern in the town, in the town
There my true love sits her down, sits her down, down
  down...
And drinks her wine as merry as can be,

George gave a big wink to Ada who was standing watching him with her arms folded.

And never, never thinks of me. Thinks of me!

A few who knew the song joined in the chorus with George.

Fare thee well, for I must leave thee,
Do not let this parting grieve thee,
And remember that the best of friends
Must part, must part.

George started the next verse.

So adieu, adieu......

He did not know the rest so he loudly "la, la'd" the tune, waving his arms to encourage others to join. And the men did for a while. Then they cheered and helped him as he shakily came down from the table. The rest of the day was a blur.

The next day Ada told him that he had acted like a fool. That she was ashamed of him. He could not tell her that during those moments of alcohol driven oblivion, he was able to forget all the things about himself that he was ashamed off. Today, they were crowding in on him even more. So, he said it was his work that made him drink and act that way, which was at least partially true.

"It's that bloody factory."

"Well find another job. I'm not having you like that."

George and Ada found two gloomy rooms back in gloomy Brentford. They both got up early to go to their work. They were back late exhausted, George stinking of tallow and feeling ill. The slow rocking ride in the sun on the dray cart, and the walk, hand in hand across the field at Heathrow, seemed like a dream.

As they sat at their table drinking tea one night, George thought about that day. He thought about the man called Alf sitting on his dray cart with those two lovely horses. He seemed happy, contented. Why wouldn't he be. Out in the air, taking his time driving the cart. Tending to the horses. "There are plenty of breweries around here ain't there?"

Ada looked sceptical. "Yeh, why?"

"I'm going to try and get a job with one of them. As a drayman. I've got experience with horses, I'm strong." He waited for Ada's approval, but she carried on drinking her tea and looking at him. After a while she said, "So that's going to be your way of getting off the beer, is it? Being a drayman?" She gave a hollow laugh. "I'm going to bed."

George was right. West London, and Chiswick in particular, had some of the biggest breweries in the country. Fuller's, Smith's, Turner's and Sich and Co. located on the Hogarth roundabout, named after the 18th century artist who painted the travails of poor people whose lives were ruined by the opiate of alcohol.

It was Sich that George tried first and successfully. The hiring man was impressed with George's knowledge and experience of horses. He had also just read a series of short stories by a young writer called Kipling. He was moved by Kipling's descriptions of hard-done-by British soldiers and wanted to give the young veteran a chance.

"Go and see Bert the charge hand. He'll get you started."

Bert was a thin, weaselly looking chap, with a small sharp nose and small sharp eyes. His whiskers accentuating the rodent feel about him. He wore a waisted woollen jacket, straight tartan-pattern trousers and a bowler hat. But it was all a little worn and tatty, and his white shirt was somewhat grubby. A paisley-patterned cravat was tied around his neck, clearly his favourite item of clothing.

George thought he was trying to be something he was not. He told him that he had been hired as a drayman. Bert laughed at him. "So, you can handle horses can you?"

"I think so."

"Well, have a go at these." He took George into a stable where two giants stood. Two of the biggest horses he had ever seen. "There we are mate, Lion and Tiger. Get them harnessed to the dray and go on your round," he smiled at George, " and the best of fucking luck mate." With that he leaned against the stable wall and watched George, with a big grin on his face.

George went up to them, he stood between them, they towered over him, he spoke to them. "I had a nice horse called Suzy," he said quietly to them. They moved nervously and snorted a bit. "We saw a lot of terrible things. I have done a lot of terrible things. But now I want a quiet life, taking barrels of beer to pubs. What about you two?"

Lion and Tiger watched him. They went quiet. He patted them both and then he cried, and he sniffed, and he wiped his eyes and they looked at him, and the charge hand said, "Fucking hell."

George harnessed them to the dray which was full of beer barrels. The charge hand gave him a list of pubs to visit and walked off looking put out. George mounted the dray, asked Lion and Tiger to go, and they did.

For the first few weeks, George was convinced that a corner had been turned. That the thoughts and dreams that had plagued him had been exorcised. It was, he told himself, being with Ada, having this job, being with the horses. That is all that was needed.

It was a Saturday. He was working in the morning but was going to watch the football with mates that afternoon. He had not slept well and had a headache. It was a gloomy day with flecks of rain falling from low, grey clouds. He had left the brewery and was taking the cart along the Chiswick High Road to deliver some barrels, first to the Packhorse and Talbot. The street was busy. He sat on the dray round shouldered and slumped. He felt cold. He had a pain in his abdomen.

Even though people were used to seeing horses pulling carts, drays and omnibuses the sight of these two towering beasts created, as it always did, a stir. As he moved along, people pointed and nodded towards Lion and Tiger and smiled. A mother with two toddlers stopped and pointed at the horses. The children became excited and jumped up and down laughing.

He idly watched the pedestrians as he trotted along. Then he saw a face among the people on the pavement. He straightened and focused on the face. The person was looking at him. The person looked grim, looked unforgiving, seemed to look through him. George kept watching, turning his neck, and was no longer looking where he was going. He knew that face. Then abruptly the horses stopped. George looked round and there was an omnibus right in front of them dropping off and picking up passengers. When he looked around the face had gone.

George was shaken. He arrived at the Packhorse and

Talbot and as usual was offered a beer after he had delivered the barrels. This time, for the first time, he accepted. "You don't look well George," the landlord said to him.

"No," he said, "Feeling rough."

He had another beer and then another and then more. When he got home, he wanted to sleep, and he did not want to go to the football with the others. He got into bed and tried to recall the face. Who was it?

The bad thoughts and feelings came tumbling back as if they were held up by a sticks and stones dam that had finally, and inevitably been breached.

From then on, he could only escape his fears by taking the beers offered on his round, but even then he couldn't escape. The feeling after was even worse. But at least he could feel numb when he was drunk.

Even when drunk the horses still listened to him, tolerated him, got him to his destinations. George would leave them bored and waiting outside a pub while he drank and talked and laughed in the bar about things that, moments later, he could not remember.

Sometimes he could not get home. He asked Lion and Tiger if he could bed with them. They agreed. So, he lay in the hay, and they gently put their giant hooves in places that would not harm him. He would wake and shout as memories overwhelmed him. But the horses would just look over their shoulders at him and then resume their chewing.

When George got home, still tired and drunk, smelling of horse dung and stale beer, Ada would gently help him down onto the floor and roll him under a table in the kitchen until he had sobered up.

The brewery kept him on despite his slow, sotted round because, it was said, he was the only man who could handle Lion and Tiger. In truth, George felt that he was the first man Lion and Tiger had felt sorry for.

12

George, Charlie, Ada, Fred and Cecil

Children inevitably came. First a boy, who, in the fashion of the time, they called George. Then, within a year Charlie, and within two more years a girl, who of course was called Ada. They were all so different. Little George was quiet. They hardly knew he was there, while Charlie was, as Ada called him, like a firecracker. Always getting into mischief and running off and being brought back by a copper holding his ear.

"You need to get this lad under control George," the copper would say.

George nodded. "Yeh, I'll give him the belt." But he never did. He never could.

Little Ada was just like her mother. She stood up for herself and put her brothers in their place. She took no nonsense. George and Charlie listened to her. Charlie would stop larking about if little Ada had had enough of it.

After a gap another boy, Fred. George would never admit it, but Fred grew to become his favourite. He was so attuned to the new century that they had moved into. He always had questions. Why are things like they are, how can things be made better? He told Ada and George that he loved them, which they found awkward as no one had said that before to anyone in the family. When he was fifteen, Fred told them he was a socialist. Neither of them knew what that was.

George did not know how to answer Fred or keep up with him. He felt he was letting the boy down. He wanted to know more so he could help the lad. But it was too late for that.

Time was passing. It was as if George was being carried along on a river, with Harry, Ali and the War swept along with him, never falling too far behind in his memory. He never felt free of his past and was never truly happy.

The face in the crowd that day. The face he could not place, would also come back at times, and haunt him. But he found a way of living with these demons, and with a growing family his sadness was tempered, at least to an extent. The drinking came in bouts rather than as a continuous daily drowning of the senses. Ada could tolerate this, and George could tolerate life.

Fred helped George tolerate life too. There was something about Fred and his easy, honest way with how he felt, that made George think hard about what he had inside him. The festering poison of mixed-up memories and guilt that he could never get to the bottom of. Fred walked tall and happy. George felt he was bent, crushed, and deformed with the legacy of confusion from his past. He wished he could start his life again. To not smell shit, but to smell something clean and clear, and something truthful and real.

They were now in their forties. Ada had become rounder with childbearing. George had become thinner. Still a strong man, but spare and slightly stooped. His hair had become thin and wispy. His beard was greying.

Unexpectedly, and late in life, came Cecil. The baby of the family, spoilt by everyone. When a small boy, he would wait for George outside the house, wait for him to come home. He would run to him and jump into his arms and say, "Can we play football?" or "Can we play cricket?" And too often George would say no.

"I'm buggered lad."

"Just play a minute."

"Tomorrow. I'll play tomorrow."

But he never did. Later he called himself, in tears, a daft bastard thinking that you get second chances, that time gives you time to try again.

Cecil always wanted to come on his round. So, on this one day, on this one round, he had Cecil by his side. By now Cecil was eight years old. He was making horse sounds as they went down the streets and pretended to hold the reigns. George stopped this one day, at the Rose and Crown. "Won't be a tick," he said to Cecil. "Don't worry the horses."

The tick was a long one. George was leaning on the bar drinking his second pint, chatting to the barman, when someone came into the pub. "Kid out here has been hurt. Anyone know him?"

Cecil was lying in the road by the horses. There was blood coming from his mouth, his nose and his ears. "One of the horses kicked him," someone said. He was alive, but he was never the same. He had fits. He could not talk. He would sit for hours doing nothing, staring, his mouth open. For George this was his punishment. He stopped drinking altogether, but he was sure there would be more pain. Harry, Rosey and Ali he thought, were getting their revenge all right.

After a year George and Ada took Cecil to the Middlesex asylum – he would be looked after there, they told themselves. They would know how to help him. Later a man in the asylum, confused and in emotional agony from the great guns of the Great War, read his poetry to Cecil.

He's gone, and all our plans
Are useless indeed.
We'll walk no more on Cotswold
Where the sheep feed
Quietly and take no heed.

Cecil loved being talked to, though there were no outward signs to show this.

George's period of being able to at least tolerate life was wearing thin. With Cecil gone he needed absolution. He desperately needed absolution. He was being punished through the ones he loved. He believed, when he thought about it, in God. But he was not religious. He wondered if he should go to church, pray, do something cosmic to change the course of his destiny. Perhaps confessing. He had heard that confessing was 'good for the soul,' but he did not think they did that in the Church of England.

So, he resolved to tell Ada everything. Well, almost

everything. He hoped that by sharing the swirl of confused memories he had bottled up inside him, by admitting culpability in other people's deaths, by saying he was guilty, guilty as charged, perhaps the weight he carried would get a little lighter. Perhaps the friends he killed would be a little more forgiving. Perhaps they would let him have some sort of life.

And so, one evening in the kitchen, the kids were somewhere, but not there. Ada was darning socks. George sat watching her. The clock ticked. He took a deep breath. "I've killed people." At least that is what he said in his head. But he did not say it out loud. He wondered what her response would be if he did.

So, he did.

"I've killed people you know."

Ada stopped what she was doing, looked at him and said, "I expect you did in that awful war. I was wondering when you would get round to talking to me about it."

They looked at each other. George thought Ada looked a little frightened as if she knew he was going to say something that would change things. There was a long silence. George looked at the sock with Ada's hand in it, now resting on her lap.

He shifted in the chair, dragged his eyes from the sock and looked at his hands, aware that Ada's gaze was on him. "Yeh but not just in the war. And it's more than that."

There was another silence as George wrestled with what he was going to say and how he was going to say it. He stood and paced up and down. Ada continued to watch him, darning needle in one hand, her other hand in the sock still resting on her lap.

"I have killed people I have…" He was not sure of the right word, so he took his cue from Fred, and he felt he had no choice now. He must say it. " I've killed people I have loved."

There was no silence this time. Ada became alarmed, "What do you mean?"

George did not know how to start this confession. "Well, first there's Harry." Then he changed his mind. "Did I tell you about the stable boy. In Alexandria. In Egypt?"

"Don't think so."

"His name was Ali. He was a stable boy, only he wasn't a boy. They just called him that. He was a very bright chap. We used to talk a lot. Well, he used to talk, and I used to listen. I looked forward to talking with him. More than any mates in my company. We would sit in the stable, late, chatting about this and that. By then, the bad feelings, that is…" George began to get anxious and lost his train of thought.

"Perhaps I should have started with Harry." George was still pacing up and down, rubbing his beard, looking distraught.

Ada was becoming more anxious. His agitation worried her. "Sit down, I'll make some tea." She started to take the sock from her hand, but George stopped her.

"No, no I have to say now. You see Ali would hold me. When no one was around, he would hold me." He was startled that he had said it. He was not sure if it was true. Not sure if his wayward memory of things was playing tricks again. But he said it.

Ada was no longer looking at him. She had her head slightly to one side looking at the floor. The hand in the sock looked rather absurd now. Like a glove puppet that had the life taken from it. "How did he hold you? I mean, oh I don't know, where did he hold you? I can't believe that I am asking you this!"

George knew, right then, that this had not gone as he had hoped.

There was silence in the room.

In the silence, George saw himself kneeling in front of Ali on the battlefield. He saw an inverted image in his mind of Ali kneeling before him in the stables. An inversion, or as George suddenly thought with a shiver, a perversion.

"I killed him," George said. "Well, l let him be killed. It's the same thing."

"'You were right to."

"No. He was not going to kill me. I knew it, but I let him die. Like I let Harry die. They both knew about me, and they died."

Ada looked puzzled. Then a little frightened. "What do you mean they knew about you?"

But he could not say what it was. Instead, he said, "Rosey drowned because of what I did to Harry. And then there was Cecil… "

Ada stood up, she was agitated, shrill and tearful, "Stop, you're getting daft thoughts. Harry and Rosey have not gone because of you. And Cecil, that was just an accident."

"But I was getting pissed in the pub!"

"Yes, you were, and I won't forgive you for that. But all this nonsense about Harry and Rosey and the Arab bloke. I don't know what you are going on about, but we are not going to talk about it again." With that she finally removed the sock from her hand and walked out of the kitchen. And George was left with a half-told, half-revealed story that again he wasn't sure was real or not. He picked up the sock and held it against his face.

From then on George and Ada never talked about that evening. It was like it never happened and the sock was never darned. Well not then.

13

Fish and Chips

They moved over the next few years, around west London and Middlesex. George got different jobs, mainly labouring work. But they saved and eventually, in 1910, rented a shop with upstairs rooms, in Brook Road, Brentford. They sold fish and chips and jellied eels. The shop was on the main street leading to Griffin Park, Brentford Football Club's ground. Brentford was a first division club so on match days they did a roaring trade.

The young George got married. Charlie became a brick layer and was earning good money. Then he got a girl, who worked in the laundry, in trouble. They had a baby who she looked after but it happened again with her. When it happened again, Ada told him he needed to do something about it. He did not look happy, but they got married. Fred helped in the shop, reading out things from the newspapers in which the fish and chips were wrapped. He looked for humorous verses or limericks or anything to make George and Ada laugh as they were so quiet and sad most of the time.

"Listen to this!"

A wonderful bird is the pelican;
His beak can hold more than his belican.
He can hold in his beak
Enough food for a week,
Though I'm damned if I know how the helican!

But he would also find more serious poems that George did not understand. One day he read from a book he borrowed from the library to George who was peeling potatoes.

It matters not how strait the gate,
How charged with punishments the scroll,
I am the master of my fate,
I am the captain of my soul.

George listened carefully and reflected that he was neither master of his fate nor captain of his soul. His life, he told himself, seemed to have gone in directions he had no control over. His mind had invented, then discarded, then reinvented versions of his life so that he was no longer sure what life he had actually lived.

George's father became too old to continue with his carting work, so he helped out at the shop. He was never much of a talker and sat quietly gutting the fish. George thought he did not look well, but it was George's mother, Eliza, who suddenly became ill and died.

George's grief was overlaid with regret that he had not talked to her more, told her more about his life and his chronic guilt and sadness. Perhaps she would have had an explanation. He never blamed her for that morning when she teased him, *Georgie Porgie, pudding and pie, kissed the girls and made them cry...*

Six months later his father, Charlie, died. People said he died, "Of a broken heart." They always said that, but George thought, for his father, it was true.

The War came and both Charlie and Fred wanted to join up. George told them nothing about what happened to him in Sudan, nothing about what it was like. He realised he still did not have the words. It seemed to him inevitable that they would experience the same horror, the fear, the screams, the blasts, hot metal, cold steel. George never thought it would be over by Christmas.

Charlie joined the Royal Engineers, Fred the Army Service Corps where he started to learn to drive a motor vehicle. He came home on leave and teased his father. "No use for horses any more dad. It's all becoming motorised now. After the war I'll be able to drive buses and lorries."

He went to war in December 1915. He was twenty years old. That same month a twenty-eight-year-old German officer, called Caesar Bauer left the port of Cattara in command of a minelaying U Boat and sailed into the Adriatic. Caesar was a handsome, strong-jawed, clean-shaven officer from an upper-middle-class military family. Fred, much as he wanted, could not grow a typical 'British Tommy' moustache. But he had pleasant features, a ready, impish smile, bright blue eyes… that's how George and Ada remembered him.

Caesar Bauer laid a string of mines outside the allied port of Brindisi in southern Italy. A month after, in January

1916, George and Ada got the news. Fred was on a troopship leaving Italy when it hit a mine and sank. He went down with the ship. His body could not be found.

George took to his bed. He thought of his son going down into the dark waters, like Harry and Rosey. He dreamt of him slipping out of his grasp like Ali. He could have done more. He could have told his sons war will be terrible, war will mean death.

George remembered a poem that Fred read out to them once. He knew he kept his favourites ones in a scrapbook. He found the book, and, after leafing through the pages he found the poem. George remembered it because it was about the sea, and death. He remembered Fred solemnly reading it when they heard about the Titanic.

A current under sea
Picked his bones in whispers. As he rose and fell
He passed the stages of his age and youth
Entering the whirlpool.

And so, George entered the whirlpool. He closed his eyes. He stayed in bed. He ignored the remonstrations of Ada who told him that she needed him to help with the shop and that he can't expect her to do it all. But George wanted to die, not to work in a fish and chip shop.

But he did not die, however much he wished for it.

14

Tea

An emaciated, stooped version of himself, prematurely aged, white hair, shuffling, finally got up and, mostly in silence, did some work. For George the story had ended. He was just counting down time now.

Until Saturday March 16th 1916.

It was the morning, the shop not yet open. Ada had gone around to a neighbour. George was sitting on a chair looking out of the shop window. He noticed a couple of daffodils poking through the dirty front yard of a house opposite. He was thinking how yellow they are compared to the grey grime of the street, how they stood out because of the absence of colour around them. Like the flowers in the desert. Like the blood in the desert.

He watched a man walking down the street in a uniform. He was looking at the numbers of the houses that were mainly on bits of old wood nailed next to the front door. He finally stopped when he saw the shop and walked up to the door. He then pulled the bell.

Even though he had watched him, George did not get up. He did not want to talk to anyone.

The man put his hand above his eyes as a sort of shield, pressed his face against the window and looked into the shop and saw George. He knocked on the window.

George looked at him. He was about George's age, mid-50s, a bit stout, a ruddy face and white whiskers, wearing a blue jacket with silver buttons. Over that a dark greatcoat. He had a white, peaked navy hat on with a badge.

With a raised voice the man said through the window, "I've come to discuss Fred with you."

There was, thought George, nothing to discuss. He is gone.

George said nothing. The man called through the window, "I should have said right away my deepest sympathy and condolences to you and your missus over the loss of your Fred."

George looked at him and carried on saying nothing.

"I'm from the war records office," the man shouted again through the window, "I deal with pensions, awards, and other payments and I thought I would pay you a visit, to explain what you are entitled to. Following the loss of your Fred."

George sighed. Perhaps he needed to listen to this man. Ada said they needed more money to pay the bills. For Ada, he decided, he would let this man in.

The man said thanks and came in. George took him to the kitchen and pointed to a chair by the table. The man said thanks again and sat down. There was a pause. George spoke for the first time. "Tea?"

"Yes, thanks."

Tea

George put the kettle on the stove and watched it. He said nothing. The man said nothing and waited.

This was not an awkward silence for George. He simply did not care about the silence. He preferred the silence.

The kettle boiled. George warmed the teapot, put two spoons of tea in, poured in the hot water, and placed it on the table to brew. He brought a tin mug and strainer from the kitchen cupboard and put those on the table alongside. "Not having one?" the man asked. George shook his head.

The man looked at George. More than that, he surveyed George's face. Then the man seemed to suddenly snap out of a trance. "Anyway," he began, "We don't usually make calls like this, it's normally all done by letter. Oh, by the way, I have the letter here, so you have it all in writing."

George nodded. The man pushed an envelope across the table towards George.

George went back to a drawer in the cupboard and found a spoon. He went back to the table and stirred the water, in the teapot. He sat down opposite the man as he did it.

"You see," the man paused, and as if he were making an effort, " I recognised the name."

They kept looking at each other during the long silence that followed. It felt strange to George. The two of them in the room. The clock ticking, water dripping from the tap. The sound of George stirring the tea, the tea water in the tea pot, round, and round. It was as if the man expected George to say something. But what?

George stopped stirring, put the strainer on the mug and poured the tea, the water was now becoming tea. He did not want the pouring to end because it meant something else would have to happen. But the tea pouring inevitably ended because the mug was full. Then George got up again and went to the scullery where a covered jug of milk was standing on a stone shelf. He brought it back and without asking, poured milk into the mug and placed the jug on the table.

The man wanted to speak but felt constrained by George's careful and slow tea making.

Then George went back to the cupboard and returned with a bowl of sugar and another spoon. A dry unused spoon. He put the bowl and the spoon on the table by the mug.

"I was a boy sailor," the man said. "Easy to join and no questions asked back then. Did all right. Came up through the ranks. When I was no good for active duty, they gave me this desk job." He paused and said again, "I recognised the name you see."

The man looked at the mug in front of him and put three spoons of sugar into it. He stirred the tea noisily and absentmindedly for a minute or two.

He took a sip of the tea because the hot water was now incontrovertibly tea and looked into the cup, and then swirled it around as if he was trying to tell a fortune from the tea leaves that had escaped the strainer. "I felt guilty about not coming back. About Rosey, but there was nothing at home for me. Mum was no saint."

There was another silence. But this time George felt different. There was nothing more he could do regarding the tea. Instead, he felt like he had slipped out of himself. Like he was standing looking at them both, looking at each other. Looking at the mug of tea.

He began to feel like all the things he had known and

done and seen, rush by, and away as if they were of no consequence.

"When I heard that people thought I had, well gone," the man continued, "I thought all right, leave it like that."

Everything George thought to be real was leaving him. Through his ears, eyes, the end of his fingers, out of his mouth. He reached over and took the man's mug of tea and took a swig from it. Despite everything, he thought, it was too weak.

Skimming mate?

Yeh all right.

I'm not working in the bloody soap factory

But we could put our money together and live somewhere, together.

You must be joking.

We push each other and wrestle. We fall on the wharf. It's stormy and grey and the river is in spate. He pushes me off and says, "bugger you then."

I walk back towards him, but he has gone. He has walked away.

"You see I recognised the name," the man in the uniform said again.

There was another pause. The man took the mug of tea back and brought it to his lips as if to drink from it but forgot and put it down.

Despite the years and the jowls George could still see the sharp enquiring nose and eyes. The potential of a mischievous look playing on his face. The man smiled.

"I saw you on the dray cart once," the man said, "I was going to wave but, well, didn't."

The moment in his life that had changed everything had changed. Everything that flowed from that moment was somehow invalid. And yet it had happened. It had damaged and hurt George. Yet the cause of it all had never existed. George could not look at the man. He stared instead at the mug.

How much really happened, George wondered. Have I dreamed a life? Am I still on the wharf?

Then the man patted George's hand, which was resting on the table.

George went to grasp the mug of tea, but the man took George's hand in his and held it.

Then he kissed George on the cheek and said,

"George."

About the Author

John Puzey was the Chief Executive of the Welsh housing charity *Shelter Cymru*. A frequent writer, broadcaster and public speaker on housing and homelessness he helped shape a range of key policies, practices, and legislation in Wales. In 2020 he published *Two Lives*, a story about two men on different sides in the First World War.

For exclusive discounts on Matador titles,
sign up to our occasional newsletter at
troubador.co.uk/bookshop